Praise for *MOTHER OF RED MOUNTAINS*

"This is historical fiction/drama at its finest. Apple An does a masterful job of infusing an atmosphere of tension and intrigue into the narrative." – **Pikasho Deka**

"Lucid storytelling. Themes of courage, fortitude, tenacity, resilience, and sacrifice are highlighted amidst the austerity, bereavement, and ordeals that the well-developed and multifaceted character went through." – **Carmen Tenorio**

"The historical details bring the setting to life, making it an essential part of the story, and teaching readers about this chaotic time in China's history." – **K. C. Finn**

"I wasn't ready for the intense emotional reactions this book brought me to. Amazingly strong FMC and the storyline was beyond encapsulating. I was transferred into this character and went through this journey with her." – **Harley Grace**

"An Epic Tale of Resilience and Courage! The blend of personal and historical storytelling is brilliantly done, and I was captivated by the vivid descriptions of China and its people. This book isn't just a historical account—it's a testament to the strength of women fighting against all odds. A must-read for anyone who loves stories of resilience, sacrifice, and love." – **Gordon C.**

"The detailed descriptions of China and its environment made it easy to picture everything vividly. The writing style is captivating and the various customs presented are fascinating." - **Alma Boucher**

"Apple An skillfully explores themes of societal prejudices, traditional family dynamics, romantic and sibling relationships, and unplanned pregnancy. What makes this book stand out is its focus on a woman's life." - **Doreen Chombu**

"If you enjoy historical fiction, this one's got it all: emotional rollercoasters, political tension, fear, struggle, and resilience. The story spotlights several strong female characters navigating loss, sacrifice, and the upheaval of a changing society. While it might be tough to picture daily life in China at times, the emotions feel universal and timeless." – **Hopper**

"You can really feel the author's personal connection—she grew up there, and it shows. The mix of history, emotion, and culture hits hard. It's packed with strong women, political drama, and real-life struggles." – **Marcell**

"Apple An's writing is both powerful and poetic, bringing historical struggles to vivid life. A masterpiece of historical fiction that reveals the extraordinary strength of ordinary women." – **ORF**

"An engaging lively and insightful view of China. I enjoyed reading this because it covers an era and culture I find fascinating. Its

emphasis is on interpersonal rather than political relations." – **Eric Engle**

"With rich storytelling and deeply emotional moments, it paints a vivid picture of resilience, sacrifice, and the human spirit's ability to endure. This poignant tale captures both the personal and political struggles of its time, making it an unforgettable read. A masterpiece for lovers of historical drama and literary fiction." – **YF**

"Jun's story really resonated with me. Her strength feels relatable, not showy, as she fights to protect her daughters through China's upheaval. I can easily imagine myself in her situation and making similar decisions, so this meant that I could feel those choices too. The scenes with the Red Guards are tense, but it's the quiet moments of love and sacrifice that had the most impact for me. I would read more from this author." – **Nathan Seal**

Awards

The 2025 American Fiction Awards: Winner for Family Saga; Winner for General Fiction; Winner for Multicultural Fiction; Finalist for Best New Fiction; Finalist for Historical Fiction

The 2025 International Book Awards: Winner for Multicultural Fiction; Finalist for Best New Fiction; Finalist for Historical Fiction

The Pencraft Spring 2025 Best Book Award: Historical Fiction

The Pencraft 2025 Best Book Award First Place Winner: Historical Fiction

The 2025 Autumn Readers' Choice Book Awards: Silver Medal for Best Adult Book

The 2025 Independent Publisher Book Awards (IPPY): Silver Medal for Multicultural Fiction

The 2025 BookFest Awards: 2nd Place for Women's Historical Fiction; 2nd for Historical Pre-2020 Fiction; 3rd Place for Historical Multi-Period Family Saga

The 2025 Next Generation Indie Book Awards: Finalist for Multicultural Fiction

The 2025 National Indie Excellence Awards (NIEA): Finalist for Asian American & Pacific Islander Fiction

The 2025 Readers' Favorite Awards: Finalist for Multicultural Fiction

MOTHER OF
RED MOUNTAINS

MOTHER OF
RED MOUNTAINS

A Novel of a Woman's Journey Through
Revolutionary China

APPLE AN

Voices Heard Publishing, LLC

Cover design by GetCovers.com

Library of Congress Control Number 2024922501

ISBNs:

eBook: 978-1-958900-15-4

Paperback: 978-1-958900-16-1

Hardcover: 978-1-958900-17-8

1st Edition, 1st Printing: December 2024

5th Printing: November 2025

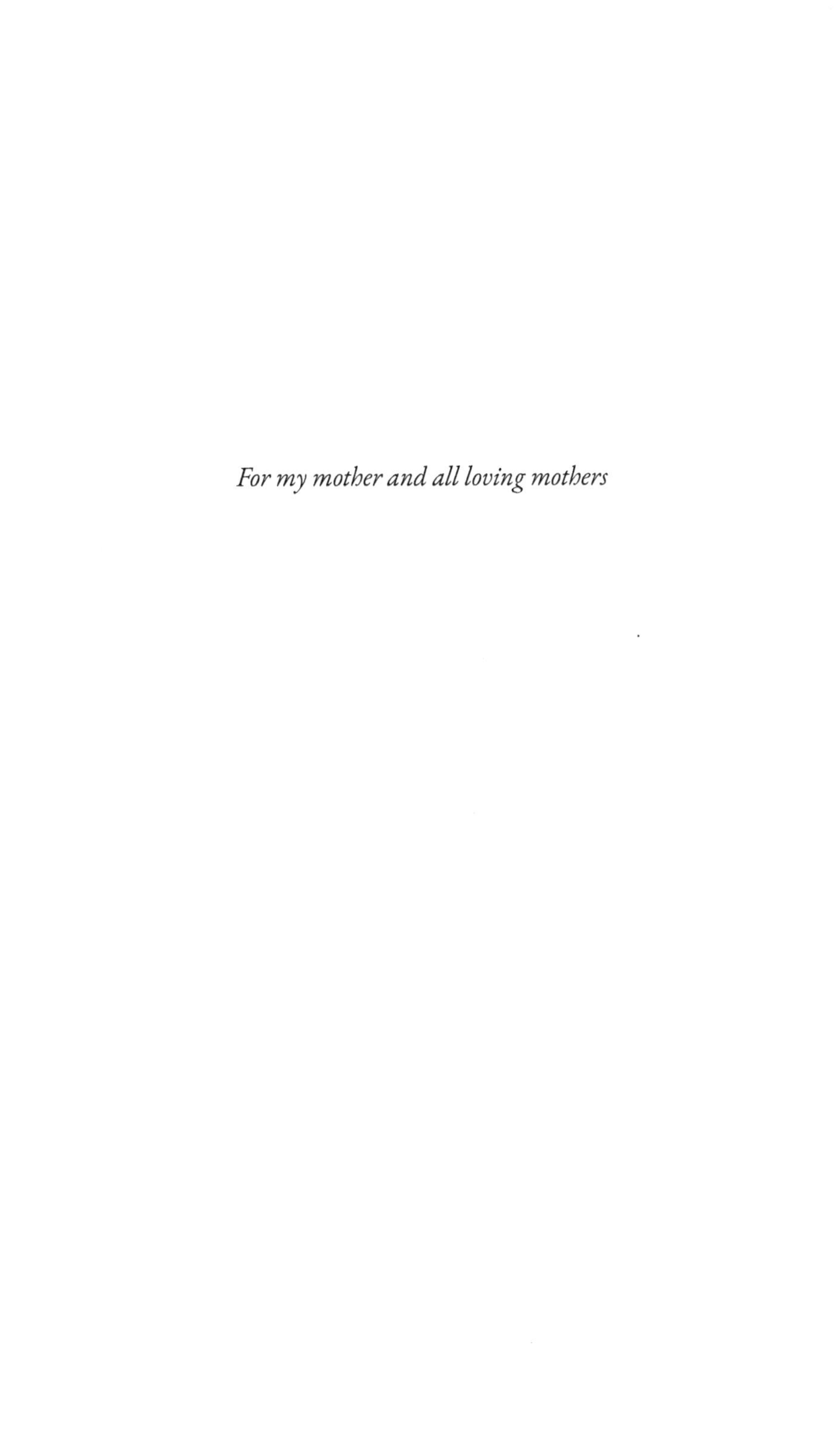

For my mother and all loving mothers

ACKNOWLEDGEMENTS

I am deeply grateful to everyone who helped make this book happen.

I thank my alpha and beta readers Bob Gates, Monica Widoff, Amber Garcia, Ann Botash, and Roxanne Bocyck. Their candid reactions and suggestions improved the book tremendously.

I owe gratitude to my editor Elisabeth Blair for her diligent, thoughtful, and skilled work on developmental and copy editing that made the book shine.

I thank my dear and brave sister Jade for her understanding and encouragement. She was instrumental in the book cover idea and provided historical verification in the stories. She continues to be a solid rock in my life.

My special appreciation goes to Jim Emery, the first and last reader of my stories, my co-conspiracist, and my sounding board.

Author's Note on Names

Chinese characters convey both meaning and sound. English transliterations into the Latin alphabet represent only the sounds of the characters—it can be especially difficult to capture the richness of Chinese names, which usually contain multiple characters with layered meanings.

This book uses the following conventions:

People's Official Names:

A man's official name could have three characters in the following order: surname, generation name, and given name. All members of the same generation within a family or clan might share a generation name. A hyphen connects the generation and given names, e.g., Xi-Chang, Xi-Dan.

Traditionally, women didn't have generation names. Some women keep their surnames after marriage, while others adopt their husband's surname.

Names for Babies and Children:

It is common practice to double syllables in names for babies or young children. For example, Lianlian and Shanshan. These doubled names can sometimes become official names when the children grow into adults.

Names for Roles:

The book may use Chinese names to refer to family roles. When these names are used by or for children, the syllables are often doubled without a hyphen. For example:

- Paternal Grandfather: Ye (Yeye)

- Paternal Grandmother: Nai (Nainai)

- Mother: Ma (Mama)

- Father: Ba (Baba)

- Uncle from father's side: Shu (Shushu)

- Older sister: Jie (Jiejie)

- Younger sister: Mei (Meimei)

Names for Places:

Chinese places—such as cities, provinces, organizations, and stores—often have multiple characters that show the type or meaning of the place. Some names become widely recognized as a single concept; for example, few people think of the literal meaning of Beijing ("Northern Capital").

For consistency, one English word is used to represent the sound of a place name, even if the original Chinese name has multiple Chinese characters. For instance, Chifeng refers to a city whose two-character name means "Red Mountains," and Xishanwan means "Valley of the West Mountains."

Contents

Part I
Chifeng, 1946–1956

1. Sunny Day 3
2. Liu Family 11
3. Rainy Day 21
4. Falling Stars 26
5. Mr. Liu's Wishes 32
6. Home No More 42
7. First Love 52
8. Scare 60
9. Prospects 65
10. Making Ends Meet 68
11. Far Away 73

Part II
Hohhot, 1956–1962

12. Blue City   79

13. School for Grownups   85

14. Unwanted Attention   90

15. Visits   98

16. Job Preparation   107

17. Job Placement   113

18. Rising Star   116

19. Hello   122

20. Goodbye   129

21. Courting   135

22. Zhou Family   143

23. Future In-Laws   151

24. Troubles   162

25. Crossroads   171

Part III

Hohhot, Jinzhou, 1963–1966

26. Expecting   183

27. Lianlian   187

28. Shanshan   194

29. Shock   199

30. Seeking Help   204

31. Young Fighter   209

32. Sisters   214

33. Promise   219

34. Red Guards   223

35. Escape   228

36. Violence   233

37. Waking Up   238

38. Choices   242

39. Gluing Pieces   248

40. Road Ahead   252

Reading Group Discussion Questions   257

Dear Reader   261

Daughter of Blue City   262
Prologue

About the Author   271

PART I

CHIFENG, 1946–1956

1

SUNNY DAY

Eleven-year-old Xiaojun sat by a huge open box near the door of her Baba's shop. She had been sorting and putting products on the shelves since early morning. When the doorbell chimed, which happened several times an hour, she'd stand up and smile at everyone coming in and going out.

It was 1946 in a major city in northeast China named Chifeng, which means "Red Mountains." Business wasn't bad, even though the country was in the middle of the Civil War.

"See you soon, Auntie!" Xiaojun said to a middle-aged woman. Her high-pitched sunny voice brightened the crowded room.

With one hand holding a bag of rice and the other patting Xiaojun's head, the woman exclaimed, "Aren't you a pretty little girl!"

Before Xiaojun sat back down, an old man with a cane in his right hand walked toward the door. His left shoulder sagged under the weight of a big black bag, and the clanging of metal sounded with each step.

"You have a good day, Grandpa! See you next time!" Xiaojun called after him with the same sunshine in her voice.

"What a doll you are. Your Baba is lucky. This place is worth visiting just to hear your voice and see your face." The old man paused, grinned at her, and walked on.

The store was quiet now. Xiaojun reached for her teacup. An over-washed shirt with a pink flower pattern loosely covered her small body. Mama had overestimated her growth rate when she made the shirt two Spring Festivals ago. The sleeves had to be rolled up to show Xiaojun's oversized hands. Mama said people with big hands would have better lives. With her short, boyish haircut, Xiaojun could move her head with ease. *So much better than pigtails tangling around my neck*, she thought, and turned her head from side to side, relishing the sense of freedom.

Her round face had a pointed chin, making her face heart-shaped, the most desirable face shape of many Chinese in her parents' generation. Of all her features, though, her eyes were the most extraordinary. Those eyes! The double eyelids inherited from her father, and her half-cherry-shaped eyes made her stand out—most people had long and narrow eyes with single eyelids. In contrast with most people's dark brown pupils, her black pupils were deep and clear, as if they led to a world filled with mystery. Many times, women in the neighborhood would say to Mama, "Xiaojun is so pretty; she looks like she comes from another world!" In response, Mama would always proudly say, "Indeed, that's the reason I named her Xiaojun, the little pretty girl—she hasn't disappointed me."

In the northern regions of China, people used "Xiao" in front of other characters to name a child. "Jun" meant pretty or handsome.

Xiaojun 小俊

Ding!

A young man entered the store.

"Welcome to Mr. Liu's! You must be new to the block?" Xiaojun stood up, her usual sunny demeanor in her voice and face.

"Yes, I'm visiting my aunt and need some parts to mend their windows." The young man stared at her for a few seconds.

Xiaojun pointed. "They're in the second row from the back."

"Aren't you too young to operate the store? Are there grownups here?" he inquired, looking around with a puzzled face. Xiaojun barely reached the height of his waist.

Before Xiaojun could answer, Mr. Liu, a man in his late 50s, came out from the back room.

"Welcome. What can I help you with?" His deep and voluminous voice stood in stark contrast to Xiaojun's.

"Oh, hi, Lao Ban (Chinese for the boss). I'm looking for some screws," said the young man.

"Come with me," Mr. Liu gestured. The young man followed those broad shoulders to the back.

Xiaojun sat down and continued shelving. She spent every morning in the store. She loved to be there, partly because she could be with Baba and she knew that made him happy, and partly because she'd get to meet people. Observing them and predicting what they might do or say was fun. Plus, she'd learn whatever news they might bring to the store. Baba had told her she didn't have to do any work, but Xiaojun liked to keep her hands busy and be useful. She couldn't stand anyone thinking badly of her. The praise from Baba and everyone else motivated her to do more and be better.

Xiaojun wiped her forehead with her sleeve and put the empty box aside. Just then, Meiling's face popped up by the door and she announced with a cheerful voice, "Time for lunch!"

From a wealthy family, Meiling was a good match for Mr. Liu's first son, Xi-Chang. According to Chinese tradition, the wife of the eldest son lived with her in-laws to help with household chores and take care of her husband's younger siblings. But Meiling's father had let the marriage go ahead on one condition for Mr. and Mrs. Liu—that Meiling wouldn't do any physical labor, domestic or otherwise.

"Not a problem. My wife is still young," Mr. Liu had said. "I have helpers around the house and at the store. Your daughter would be the last person to work on anything."

With two pigtails, Meiling had a fuller figure: round face, round shoulders, round arms, and round hips. When the matchmaker mentioned her, the first thing Mr. Liu asked was how big she was—her physical shape. Mr. Liu was happy with his own wife's body size. Tiny girls, however, would have trouble giving birth.

"Oh, don't you worry! She can bear children for sure. She has wide hips," the matchmaker assured him. After Mr. and Mrs. Liu had already declined five other girls, the matchmaker wanted this one to work.

Xiaojun still remembered the wedding day. Several young men unloaded boxes after boxes from four horse-drawn carts, along with several large pieces of furniture. The unspoken message was that the bride's rich parents adored her, so her in-laws should too.

"Is my brother home from school for lunch?" asked Xiaojun, knowing what the answer would be.

Since the wedding, Meiling had been greeting Xi-Chang every day on the corner of the street when he came home for lunch or in the afternoon. At 16, Xi-Chang was still in school. Happily married and adoring his wife, he grew worried one afternoon when he didn't see Meiling by the street corner. Rushing home, he was told Meiling was having "the day of the month" and was hurting badly. For the rest of that day, he didn't leave her side.

"Yes, he's home and eating lunch now. You'd better hurry before the food gets cold." Meiling used her right hand to brush off a piece of hair from Xiaojun's forehead. Being the only girl at home, she'd always wanted a sister. Xiaojun was a nice playmate. Even though they were several years apart, Meiling didn't pay much attention to their age gap.

Xiaojun went to the back. "Baba, it's lunchtime."

Mr. Liu raised his head and said, "You two go now. I'll come as soon as I finish helping this young man."

Xiaojun unrolled her sleeves and followed Meiling to the family compound, not far behind the store.

***

Xi-Chang and Meiling lived in the East House on one side of the yard. Xiaojun used to visit daily before Meiling moved in. Since then, Meiling had decorated the place to her own taste and displayed many items she'd brought from her parents' home, including fancy furniture and nicer bedding. Xiaojun got to visit only when Meiling invited her.

Xiaojun liked Meiling—she was nice, not a picky eater, and not easily irritated. She'd listen to whatever Xiaojun was talking about and never interrupted her. She treated Xiaojun as a peer, not a child. And she'd braided Xiaojun's hair—until Mrs. Liu cut it after Xiaojun's persistent requests.

Still, Xiaojun felt uneasy and jealous because her brother spent much more time with Meiling than with her. He now spent all his time after school with Meiling in their East House.

"It's not fair. He was my brother first!" Xiaojun complained to Mama once.

"Married people spend more time together," said Mama.

"But I get to spend time with Baba and you don't always keep him to yourself," countered Xiaojun.

"It's different. You're Baba's girl. Wait until your brother and Meiling have children. Then they'll be different, too," Mrs. Liu said reassuringly.

Mrs. Liu was the cook of the family. It never bothered her to prepare three meals a day for the family of seven: herself, Mr. Liu, their two sons Xi-Chang and Xi-Dan, two daughters Xiaojun and Xia, and daughter-in-law Meiling. The boys were no help at all. When Mrs. Liu was too busy to go by herself, she'd send Xiaojun to the market to buy groceries. Xiaojun would bring back the right stuff while spending the least amount of money. Helping Baba with the bookkeeping made Xiaojun good with numbers, and she had a keen sense of money's worth.

Mr. Liu came home for lunch. "Junjun, you take a break this afternoon." He was the only one who called Xiaojun that. "There's no need for you in the store."

"Come to our room after the nap," Meiling invited Xiaojun.

Everyone took a brief nap after lunch. Afterward, they'd each attend to their own business during the afternoon: Students

Xi-Chang and Xi-Dan would go back to school; Mr. Liu would go back to the store; and Mrs. Liu would take Xia to get water for laundry or whatever household chores she had to do.

Xiaojun knew Meiling had a collection of books in the East House. This had excited Xiaojun—and made her envious. She had no books because she couldn't read. Mr. Liu kept saying, "You learn more in the store than in school." Her parents had no books either. Mama could only recognize her name. Before the wedding, Xiaojun had never seen books in Xi-Chang's room besides his textbooks. She had, however, seen a stack of old books in Xi-Dan's room, but he always chased her out whenever she sneaked into his place.

Inside the East House, Xiaojun picked up one book and flipped through it. Besides words, there were drawings. She guessed the meaning of some of them, and looked at Meiling with beautiful, smiling eyes.

Meiling knew the look. "Would you like me to read to you?"

This was one of those few moments she considered herself useful or even superior.

Xiaojun nodded and jumped onto the edge of the kang to sit next to Meiling, who took the book from Xiaojun and opened it. She read smoothly, her voice rising and falling animatedly. At the end of each page, she let Xiaojun turn the page eagerly.

Time seemed to vanish.

"Wow!" Xiaojun exclaimed after Meiling had finished reading the last page. Taking the book in her hands, Xiaojun thumbed through it page by page. She pointed at the words on the cover and asked for two words she hadn't learned from Meiling yet.

This was one of the few reasons she was glad Meiling had joined the family. She wished she could read like Meiling. The stories in the books were fascinating and she could see herself enjoying them very much. But the ability to read, Xiaojun thought, would be a superior skill in life.

2

LIU FAMILY

Mr. Liu had been born in Shandong Province in 1890. The Chinese famine of 1906–07 forced many people from the southern regions, such as the Anhui and Jiangsu areas, to move to the middle regions, including Shandong. Mr. Liu's family had run out of options to make a living, and his father took him to migrate to the northeast region. He would never see his mother and big sister after that, and within two years, his father became ill and died.

Young Mr. Liu moved around to find odd jobs to support himself. After a few years, he settled in Chifeng. Not only did people seem kinder there, but there were more opportunities. The malnutrition in his early life hadn't seemed to affect his growth. He was a strong young man, taller than most men in his generation, with broad shoulders and a square-shaped face, plus those double eyelids rare among Chinese. He also had a gentle temperament. Altogether, he was a handsome and manly man who became well-liked, even popular.

When a family had no sons but only daughters, they could "recruit" a man to marry their daughter and live with them. Any children from that marriage would carry the mother's surname.

At 24, Mr. Liu became the family-blood-carrying son (in-law) by marrying the only daughter of his widower boss, a shop owner, who shared the common surname Liu.

When his father-in-law retired, the younger Mr. Liu took over the shop. Although he never went to school, he was a quick study. He had no trouble managing all aspects of the business. That he was handsome and well-liked also helped him earn an excellent reputation and make connections. The business prospered.

Mr. Liu's father-in-law had owned a two-room house behind the shop and some land surrounding the area. Two years after joining the family, Mr. Liu expanded the small house into a compound with four sections and a courtyard. In Chinese tradition, principal houses, or the houses with the highest value, should sit on the north side and face the south. Mr. Liu's North House had three rooms: one for sitting or gathering, one for cooking and dining, and one bedroom with a big kang. A kang was a built-in bed made of bricks and mud that covered a significant portion of a bedroom for the entire family to sleep in. It had to be heated by the cooking stove in the cooking room daily to ensure people didn't sleep in a cold kang.

The two rooms on the east side were called the East House, which had a separate entry and the potential for cooking or heating its kang. Mirroring the East House was the West House. On the south side was the Gate House. It had an arched gate in the middle and a room on each side of the gate. Mr. Liu and his wife lived in the North House. His father-in-law lived in the East House. He rented the rest of the houses for people he hired. The courtyard was where clothes were laundered and hung to dry and where children would play—though Mr. Liu and his wife had no children. There was a pressurized well (which had a handle that needed pumping to get water out) toward the corner between the North House and the West House.

Unfortunately, Mr. Liu's father-in-law died from an illness, and his wife's death followed soon after. By then, Mr. Liu's shop had become the only one of its kind in this part of the city. He had learned the hard way to not stock anything perishable. If a product was hardy, long-lasting, and commonly used, he would have it in the shop.

Two years after his wife's passing, Mr. Liu was ready for another wife. Through a matchmaker, at age 40, he found a young lady from a working family of eleven children. The marriage proposal was highly desirable for the young lady and her family. A sole wife was the most respected. Other roles could be an additional wife (men could marry more than one woman), a concubine (not considered a member of the family even though she might live with and belong to a man), or a mistress (who may have relationships with more than one man). The families of these women would carry the same respect as these women carried. Mr. Liu made sure his offer was higher than anyone else could make.

At 18, the new Mrs. Liu was quite a beauty by any standards. Slightly shorter than her husband but much taller than her peers, she had a ballerina's body with a straight back, long arms, and long legs. She moved as gracefully as a dancer, airy and flowing. Her abundant black hair was often braided and drawn up at the back of her head, making her long neck even longer and more gorgeous. Her rosy cheeks could warm up a room and everyone in it.

And Mrs. Liu was more than just eye candy. She carried out her domestic duties with ease: cooking, sewing, cleaning, and childbearing and raising. The only thing she refused to do was to appear in her husband's shop or interfere with any part of the business. "The store is his world," she'd always say. Most shoppers hardly ever saw her.

Four children had kept her busy. Her firstborn came in 1930 before the first anniversary of her wedding. Mr. Liu wanted to have a generation name for his sons, just as most reputable families would do for their blood carrying hairs. After consulting with a scholar, he and Mrs. Liu decided on the word Xi, which means happiness. They named their first born Xi-Chang.

A handsome and mild-natured boy, X-Chang had been the apple of Mrs. Liu's eye since he was a young boy. In a way, Xi-Chang was secretly more important to her than her husband. Her affectionate glance frequently alighted on Xi-Chang, and she'd save delicious and rare food for him and him only. The most noticeable signs that she was protective of her oldest son were her strong objections against several girls the matchmaker offered as potential brides for him. Even Mr. Liu thought her reactions were unreasonable—he thought many of those girls would be fine choices for their son's bride.

The second son, Xi-Dan, came two years after Xi-Chang. Also handsome in his own way and eventually even taller than his brother, Xi-Dan was naughty and carefree, the opposite of Xi-Chang. Full of ideas, he'd often do things behind his parents' backs and deny it when caught. As a result, Xi-Dan got many complaints from his teachers and the grownups in the neighborhood. "That boy of Mr. Liu's," they'd say, shaking their heads and sighing. Half of the time,

Mrs. Liu didn't see such things as bad. To her, Xi-Dan was a good boy—not as good as Xi-Chang, but better than the neighborhood boys. Mrs. Liu became a safe shield for Xi-Dan whenever Mr. Liu lost his temper with him.

"Ma Maaa..." Xi-Dan would cry, rushing to his Mama. His eyes were tear-filled and his voice soft, as if he'd been the victim of a crime. He wouldn't dare face his father's red face and flaring nostrils, a wooden stick in his hand.

"You go easy on him. He's a boy. Boys need to make mistakes and learn from them," Mrs. Liu would insist, pulling Xi-Dan behind her.

"You! You're spoiling him." Mr. Liu would lower his voice and turn away. That would be the harshest thing he'd say to his wife. He truly adored her and considered himself the luckiest man in the world to be married to her. She gave him two sons, which made him love her even more.

As it happened, two girls came into their lives, too. But what adventures they brought.

***

Xiaojun was born in 1935, three years after Xi-Dan. It was love at first sight for Mr. Liu. This young, precious, vulnerable little being was like nothing he had ever seen or felt before. Though he had adored each of his two wives, this little girl was so different in so many ways. Day by day, as Xiaojun grew bigger, Mr. Liu's love for her grew exponentially. Not only was she the most beautiful girl he'd ever seen, but Xiaojun was the smartest among all his children and compared with other children he'd known.

She was quick to learn, observant and sensitive. Through her eyes, he learned and noticed things he'd never known before—about people, ideas, and feelings. Mr. Liu couldn't help but wonder if Xiaojun was the reincarnation of a wise person from another time. He treated Xiaojun partially as a darling daughter and partially as a peer. He'd discuss business matters with her as if she was a grown-up, before she'd even turned ten years old. And much to his delight, Xiaojun loved to be around him and talk about anything and everything related to the shop.

In 1938, when Xiaojun was three, Mrs. Liu was seven months pregnant. A virus was spreading through the city—a rare eye disease that had affected many children. Horrific news came from all corners of the neighborhood when people visited Mr. Liu's shop, about which child had been the latest to lose eyesight in one or both eyes.

Xiaojun's left eye was itchy. She couldn't help but rub it from time to time, even though Mama told her never to do so. In a few days, the itchiness intensified, and she had trouble seeing clearly. Mrs. Liu became worried. "We need to take her to the doctor. We can afford it, can't we?"

Many children who had lost their eyesight had been from families with limited income.

"I've already sent the request. Dr. Suzuki can see her tomorrow," declared Mr. Liu as he paced back and forth. He was even more worried than his wife, but he didn't show it; real men didn't show their emotions.

Mrs. Liu's concern turned to anger. "A Japanese doctor? Aren't we supposed to stay away from the Japanese as much as possible? Haven't we heard enough horrible stories?"

"Yes. But he's the best doctor in town. I've heard good things about him. Maybe he's different from those soldiers. And he accepted my request, saying he'd heard good things about me, too."

Dr. Suzuki and his wife lived in another part of the city. He'd originally come as a doctor accompanying the Japanese troops when they occupied Northeast China in 1932. Soon after, he'd retired from the army and settled to practice medicine in Manchukuo, a puppet state created by Japan that comprised the northeastern regions of China.

Dr. Suzuki examined Xiaojun and prescribed medicine and treatment. A few days later, he checked on Xiaojun. Her condition was better.

"She should be fine," Dr. Suzuki assured Mr. and Mrs. Liu. He nodded at Mrs. Liu. "I see you're expecting another child. And your daughter Xiaojun is so pretty."

"Yes, I am. How many adorable kids do you and your wife have?" Mrs. Liu asked politely.

"We don't have any, although we love kids." It was a frank admission from someone who barely knew them.

Mrs. Liu felt the obligation to continue. "You must want a son, as is our custom here."

To her surprise, Dr. Suzuki said, "My wife and I are neutral about a baby's gender. We welcome both."

As Mrs. Liu's delivery date approached, she felt extremely unsettled.

"This pregnancy differs from the other three. Something about this baby doesn't feel right. Maybe we should visit a fortuneteller," she suggested to her husband.

"If you wish. We can go tomorrow. Lao Zhao can cover the shop."

Lao Zhao had been with the store for years. He was a reliable, middle-aged man who lived in the Gate House with his wife. They had no children.

Close to the shop was a temple which Mr. and Mrs. Liu visited from time to time. Although they weren't religious, like many others, they'd visit to make a wish or to draw a stick for their fortune.

The fortuneteller's face became stiff when he saw the stick Mrs. Liu had drawn.

"You can tell us what you saw. We can take it," Mr. Liu said calmly.

"This stick says this baby you're carrying, umm, well, it might be a force to destroy your wealth and prosperity." The teller said slowly at first, then finished up quickly.

"Is that so?" Mr. Liu asked in a tone of disbelief.

"That explains why I've been so irritated lately," Mrs. Liu exclaimed. "Let's go home now."

"There's more," the teller said, then hesitated.

"Good or bad?" Mr. Liu asked.

"Umm, well, umm, it's, well..."

"Never mind. Thank you for your service." Mr. Liu passed a coin to him. "Keep the change."

"This is too much. Let me..." The teller fumbled through his packet.

Mr. Liu lifted his wife from the bench and walked out of the temple.

At night, Mr. and Mrs. Liu stayed up late. It was hard to brush off their concerns about what the fortuneteller had said.

"It seems we can't keep this baby," Mrs. Liu said sadly, and continued, "Fortunately, we have two boys already."

Mr. Liu paced back and forth. He felt a responsibility toward his wife and three children and for this baby as well.

"Giving babies away is a common practice," Mrs. Liu continued. "We've seen many of our acquaintances do it for all kinds of reasons. Not destroying the family's wealth is a good reason." Somewhere inside her, she didn't believe this baby would be part of the family.

Mr. Liu said, "True. We need to find a decent family so this baby can have a good life."

Mrs. Liu's face lit up. "What about Dr. Suzuki? They want a child regardless of the gender. He seems like a kind man. He saved Xiaojun's eye. We could never repay him for his skills and kindness. He would be a great Baba for this baby."

"Let me check with him. We don't know what kind of person his wife is."

A meeting between the Lius and the Suzukis happened. They agreed the Lius would never visit the baby. If they met by chance, they would never reveal their relationship to the child.

When Mrs. Liu gave birth, the labor was arduous. After nineteen hours, the midwife finally announced, "It's a girl!"

Mrs. Liu struggled to sit up with the support of a pile of pillows and whispered, "Can I take a quick look at her?"

"No, you shouldn't. I'll be right back after giving her to Mrs. Suzuki," said the midwife, wrapping up the baby with a blanket.

"Listen," Mrs. Liu said in a weak voice. "I just want a quick look at her before she's gone forever."

The midwife hesitated. But she couldn't bear to see Mrs. Liu's painful, pleading eyes.

"Only one glance. You promise me."

And that was it. Xia could never leave Mrs. Liu's side, ever. "My baby girl," she said.

Mr. Liu settled the matter with Dr. Suzuki. Soon after, the doctor and his wife left the city. The rumor was that they had returned to Japan so his wife could have a stable and familiar place to have a baby of their own.

3

RAINY DAY

One afternoon, two months after Xi-Chang and Meiling's wedding in 1946, Xiaojun closed the accounting book. It had been her duty to balance the sheet for so long that she couldn't remember when she'd first started. Baba trusted her and sometimes did not even check the numbers after she finished them. "Just give me a summary of how we're doing," he'd say. Today, she'd finished earlier than planned.

Stepping out into the yard, Xiaojun let the drops of rain fall on her face. She didn't mind gray days. To her, this was what nature was about, and she welcomed all weather and seasons.

What's Meiling doing? Maybe we could read another book, and she could teach me a few more words.

She walked to the East House and tapped on the door. No sound. She tapped again. She was sure Meiling was in there. *Where else would she be on this rainy day?* She tapped a third time and waited.

A few moments later, Meiling opened the door. Her hair was messy. Her face had an expression of not knowing where she was.

"Sorry, I didn't mean to wake you up from your nap," Xiaojun apologized, but also felt puzzled. It was way past the usual nap time.

"What do you want?" Meiling asked with a hollow voice, unlike her usual upbeat tone. Her gaze was unfocused. There was no sign of her habitual smile.

"Oh. I was wondering what you're up to... Are you alright?" Xiaojun was alarmed because Meiling looked and acted like a stranger.

"Fine. Go away." Meiling shut the door in Xiaojun's face.

Xiaojun's mouth opened, and her jaw dropped. She sprinted into the North House and found Mrs. Liu sewing.

"Mama, something's wrong with Meiling. Come quickly."

They rushed to the East House, opened the door without knocking, and stepped in.

Meiling was sitting in a chair next to the dresser and turned to them with a dreamy expression on her face. Her mind was clearly somewhere else. It was hard to tell if she even recognized them. On top of the dresser, there was a cute little bottle with round shoulders and artistic images. It was so tiny Meiling could have hidden it inside her closed hand.

Mrs. Liu picked up the bottle and brought it to her nose. Her face changed from worry to disgust to anger. She put down the bottle, grabbed Xiaojun's hand, and stepped out of the room, saying nothing.

Xiaojun struggled within the tight grasp and asked, "Mama?"

They were in the yard now.

"Stay away from her, hear me? Stay away!"

Mrs. Liu said it as if Meiling had infectious disease.

Dinner that night was normal in every way. Xiaojun couldn't see any difference in Meiling. Her cheeks were rosy, her hair neat, and her eyes shone. Her smile was as lovely as usual, she talked in her normal upbeat tone, and she picked up food with her chopsticks and put it into Xi-Chang's bowl, just as she did every day. It was like nothing had happened. But Xiaojun noticed Mama's tense body posture and saw her sneaking glances at Meiling from time to time.

The next day, Xi-Chang was called to his parents' room after breakfast. Xiaojun knew something was up because he ended up staying there for a long time—he'd already missed the start of the school day. Meiling was pacing back and forth in the dining room, wringing her hands. Usually, she'd have walked with Xi-Chang to the street corner to say goodbye for the morning.

When Xi-Chang came out, his face was red, and his eyes were filled with fire. He pulled his belt off as he walked toward Meiling.

Meiling's face changed from worry to horror. Without a word, Xi-Chang whipped the belt at her. She turned and ducked, putting her hands over her face, then made a loud anguished sound when the whip landed on her back. The next one landed on the top of her head.

Xiaojun couldn't believe her eyes. Her mild-tempered big brother had done nothing remotely close to this. As she put her hands over her mouth, Mr. Liu stepped in and grabbed the belt in the air. By now, Meiling had collapsed on the floor, sobbing loudly.

For the next two days, Xi-Chang slept in Xi-Dan's West House. Meiling never left her room. Mrs. Liu was the only person to visit her. Food trays appeared untouched when they were taken out. After Xiaojun came home from the store, Mrs. Liu would ask her to empty and clean the night chamber and put it back outside the door of the East House. When she did, Xiaojun would hear Meiling crying inside.

On the third day, Xiaojun woke up to the loud clamor of people shouting and heavy footsteps. She ran out into the yard. Mr. Liu was telling Lao Zhao, "Get a doctor!" Xi-Chang sat on the threshold of the West House, his hands over his lowered head. Xi-Dan was sitting next to him, staring intensely at the East House, the door of which was wide open. Xiaojun ran into the room and saw Mrs. Liu using a towel to clean Meiling's face—there was white stuff coming out of Meiling's mouth. Her face was as pale as white paper and her eyes were closed. On her pillow lay bunches and bunches of long, black hair—no longer connected to her head! One bunch of hair was clutched tightly in her right hand.

"Mama!" Xiaojun was beyond shocked.

"Go attend to your sister," Mrs. Liu waved her hand. There was fear in her eyes.

Xiaojun hesitated. She wanted to know more, but she didn't want to upset Mama, who seemed upset enough already. She returned to the North House and pulled the crying little girl into her arms. Grabbing some food and putting it in Xia's hand, she led Xia to the door and sat with her on the threshold.

A doctor came. Not too long later, Xiaojun heard Mama screaming like crazy. She had never heard Mama scream.

Days later, Xiaojun saw Meiling's parents for the second time. The sadness on their faces was heartbreaking.

Xiaojun was heartbroken, too, and filled with guilt and regret. Not only had she lost a friend, but she wondered whether she was the one to blame for Meiling's death. If she hadn't knocked on Meiling's door on that dreadful rainy afternoon, she wouldn't have discovered Meiling's condition. If she hadn't reported it to Mama,

Mama wouldn't have found out that Meiling was using drugs. Then Mama wouldn't have told Xi-Chang about the danger of the entire family going bankrupt because of the ravages of one family member's addiction. And Xi-Chang wouldn't have beaten and humiliated Meiling in front of everyone. If she had never given Meiling the rat poison two weeks ago when Meiling said she'd seen a mouse, then Meiling wouldn't have been able to swallow it.

From that day on, Xiaojun hated rainy days.

4

FALLING STARS

One month after Meiling died, the entire family said goodbye to Xi-Chang, and then watched him get onto the back of a military truck. Unable to bear living at home anymore, Xi-Chang had joined Chiang Kai-Shek's National Army to fight in the Civil War.

Two months later, they received Xi-Chang's first and only letter.

> "We've been traveling without being told where we're going. Today, we're resting in a small village. All is well so far. I'll write again when I get the chance."

He didn't leave a return address.

Xiaojun's heart ached every time she thought about her favorite brother, which was daily. Not knowing if he was still alive was worse than knowing Meiling was dead.

Life at home changed. More gray hair showed up at Mr. Liu's temples. He became quiet and his face was hard to read. He spent more time at the store and often sat by himself, doing nothing. It

Mr. Liu asked the young man to pretend to be Xi-Chang. The uniformed young man sat on the kang by Mrs. Liu, calling "Mama, Ma. I'm back."

But Mrs. Liu's eyes didn't open.

The night after Mrs. Liu's burial, Xiaojun sat in the yard by herself. She looked up at the sky and wondered which star was Mama's. She wrapped her arms around her chest as if trying to cope with the cold that filled her from the inside out. There was an emptiness in her heart she was experiencing for the first time. She couldn't imagine a life without Mama. Not merely because of practical matters like cooking, sewing, cleaning, telling the kids what to do, etc. It was also the belief Xiaojun had always had in her as a place of safety. If anything bad happened to her, Mama would be the one to go to, to get resolution, comfort, or protection. Mama's tall and vibrant figure was always there in the home, either in front of Xiaojun, in her peripheral vision, or in the back of her mind.

How could Mama disappear forever? What will happen to the family now? To Baba, to Xia? To everyone else? To me?

Xiaojun kept looking up at the sky. There were so many stars, some shiny and some dim.

Maybe I should aim to be a shiny star. Yes, I should. I'll help the dim stars get brighter. I'll stay up there for as long as possible, so my family won't be heartbroken, missing me.

5

MR. LIU'S WISHES

The establishment of the new People's Republic of China in 1949 brought a lot of changes at lightning speed. Mr. Liu was overwhelmed. *Maybe I'm getting old,* he thought.

He wanted his children to take over the store and the care of the family before it was too late. With no news from Xi-Chang, Xi-Dan was the only son left. He knew Xi-Dan wouldn't be the candidate. But a son was a son. They had responsibilities to their families.

Mr. Liu realized he had not received any complaints from the teachers or the neighbors about Xi-Dan for a long time now, maybe since Xi-Chang had left home. He carefully examined Xi-Dan, who seemed to have grown several centimeters taller than the last time he'd paid close attention to him. He knew Xi-Dan went to school daily and stayed in his room apart from mealtimes. Sometimes, music drifted out of his room, though Mr. Liu couldn't tell what instrument it was from. The one and only time Xi-Dan had asked his father for something was for money to buy eyeglasses, saying he couldn't see very well, and his allowance wasn't enough to purchase such an expensive item. Xi-Dan seemed to have matured.

"Do you have any plans to help me run the store once you finish school?" Mr. Liu asked one day right after dinner, before Xi-Dan slipped away.

"Ba, I've been meaning to discuss this with you. I want to be a teacher. To do that, I need to attend a teacher's preparation school."

"A teacher? What does school do for anyone? People learn no practical skills at school. Look at you—you don't help with the store or the family. You play music, but that has no practical value. You can't even help Xiaojun figure out discrepancies in the store's accounting book. Now you want to waste other children's lives by teaching them?" Mr. Liu's disappointment and disapproval were palpable.

"Ba, school makes people smart."

"Yeah? Show me the evidence."

Xi-Dan scratched his head. It had always been difficult to communicate with his dad. Well, not only his dad. The only family member he could talk with was Xia. Even Xiaojun was hard to talk to.

"Tell you what. You can continue your schooling for whatever you want to do, and I'll support you—as long as you can give me a grandson before you start your new school."

"But Ba, I'm too young to get married."

"Says who?"

"You were 24 when you first got married. I'm still young."

"Yes, but it was because no one provided for me, and I had to struggle through life by myself. Look at you—you never worry about your next meal or how to put a roof over your head. Plus, your brother got married at 16." His voice faded and he turned his head to hide his sadness.

Xi-Dan paused. He missed his brother, too. He wanted to help the family now that Xi-Chang had disappeared, but he couldn't find a way his dad might approve of. Staring at his father's slightly arched back and gray hair, he realized the duty of carrying the family's bloodline fell on his shoulders.

"Ba. I'll get married, for the family's sake."

Less than one year later, in 1950, Xi-Dan's wife Peifang gave birth to Tiger, a big, healthy boy. Peifang was the eldest of six children from a family with barely enough resources to buy food. Mr. Liu thought she must be capable domestically, one of the main reasons he had favored her over other girls. However, she got pregnant immediately and her pregnancy put her in bed a lot because of complications. She had hardly any time to help with any house chores. Mr. Liu figured as long as Xi-Dan liked her, it should still work out. But, she had little to earn her husband's affection: a plain look, a boring personality, illiterate and almost proud of it, and a lacked knowledge of—or interest in—anything outside of the humdrum of daily life. Two months after Tiger was born, Xi-Dan moved to Chengde to start his vocational school for teachers. Chengde was several hours away by long-distance buses, and he visited home only during holidays or school breaks.

***

Mr. Liu was relieved there was a boy in the family. However, the family business still had an uncertain future. He thought about Xiaojun, wishing fervently that she was a boy. She had all the qualifications to be a good businessperson and carry on the family business affairs. After Mrs. Liu had died, Xiaojun had built a reputation as a reliable contributor to the running of the shop. People still talked about something she'd done the first time she'd picked up products from a merchant.

"Ba, you can't leave the store now, and we agreed to pick up the merchandise. I'll go with Lao Zhao," she offered. She had turned 12 two weeks before.

Out of necessity, Mr. Liu agreed, giving her some brief instructions and a piece of paper with a list of drawings and numbers.

The merchant was surprised to see Lao Zhao, who could only do manual labor and couldn't read or even communicate clearly.

"If Mr. Liu is so tied up, and my condolences on the passing of his wife, we can hold the goods for another week," said he.

"No need. I'm here to pick them up." Xiaojun stepped forward and presented the list.

Until that moment, the merchant hadn't even noticed her. With a slim and short frame and boyish haircut, Xiaojun had a determined expression in her dark eyes. She betrayed no hint of emotion on her pretty, heart-shaped face.

"Oh, little girl, it must have been a hard journey to make it here on a three-wheeled cart. Shouldn't you be playing at home?"

"Can you check the list and put your fingerprint at the bottom after loading all the goods?" Xiaojun was all business.

The merchant looked at her in disbelief. He felt partly embarrassed and partly amused.

Holding the list, he picked out various goods for Lao Zhao to load.

"Well, here are all the goods. If you agree, we can both put our fingerprints on the paper for you to take home." He passed the list to Xiaojun, folded his arms, and stood aside.

Xiaojun had been inspecting the goods as Lao Zhao loaded them.

"Mister, two pieces are missing for this product and three are missing for this one. You also gave us one extra for this product." Xiaojun pointed at the paper.

"What? Are you sure? Can you count?" The man stared at her. "Just so you know, your Baba trusts me and has never counted."

"I don't know you and have no reason to trust you. Do you want to check again yourself?"

"No need. You're right. I was testing you. Here are the rest of the missing ones. Your Baba is lucky. See you next time."

Mr. Liu smiled as he recalled that story. Word had gotten around, and no one had ever dared trick Xiaojun again.

His thoughts continued on the future of the family and the store. *Well, I was a family-blood-carrying son-in-law. I don't mind if Xiaojun marries someone and takes over the family business, regardless if the young man carries the family name or not.*

But Xiaojun nipped that idea in the bud. "No, Ba. I don't want to get married. I want to stay in school. Getting married means I have to quit school," she said firmly.

Soon after Mrs. Liu died, eight-year-old Xia had become a loose goose, causing trouble at home or playing long hours outside. Mr. Liu sent her to school. However, two years later, Xia was still in the first grade. Mr. Liu eventually found out that Xia hardly ever actually attended classes. Instead, she'd leave home after breakfast, hide her schoolbag, and play with friends until it was time to go home for meals.

Out of desperation, and because Xiaojun's constant begging to go to school had worn down his resolve, Mr. Liu agreed to let Xiaojun start school—if she could keep Xia in school as well. Three years after Mrs. Liu died, Xiaojun had been 14 and Xia 11, and they'd begun school together. Now it was 1950, and Xia, who was quite bright, had moved to 2nd grade. Xiaojun, who'd already known a lot of materials, had skipped a grade and was now in 3rd grade.

Mr. Liu knew Xiaojun loved school and was good at it, but he never believed schooling was going to be of help. He said to Xiaojun, "You know girls don't need to go to school."

"It's not about needing to go to school. I want to go to school. I love school."

"But eventually, you'll marry."

"Let it be later. I'm not ready to settle down. Look at Peifang. I couldn't stand a life like hers." Xiaojun regretted it as soon as those words came out of her mouth. "Ba, what I meant is..."

Mr. Liu waved his hand. "No need to explain. I know you, Junjun. You always set your sights on climbing to the very top of any mountain in front of you. I know you'll fly high and far. Take Xia with you."

"Ba, don't worry too much about the family or the shop," Xiaojun reached out for his hand, and he grabbed hers.

"I know you love school," he said. "I also know you love the shop. It's too tiring for you to spend this much time in the store after school. What do you think about selling it?"

"What?!" Xiaojun was stunned. The store had been her playground for as long as she could remember.

"I'm not young anymore. I am 60 now," Mr. Liu sighed. His right hand stretched out to support his lower back.

"The recent changes related to land reform and family classification are overwhelming. It's hard to say what might come."

Xiaojun nodded. She had noticed some side-eyes from people when she went with Lao Zhao to pick up the merchandise.

Mr. Liu continued, "I've saved enough for all of us. If we sell it now, we might still get a good deal before the situation deteriorates. You work daily in the store, so I wanted to discuss this with you first."

"But we've owned the store for so long."

"Yes, but all things have a beginning and an end. Endings aren't always bad, as long as there's a good reason."

"But what will you do without the store?" Xiaojun couldn't imagine what her father's days would be like.

"I'll play with Tiger and visit and chat with friends. There should be plenty for me to do." Mr. Liu couldn't quite picture anything beyond that.

Xiaojun thought for a long while. Her father was right. Not all endings were bad. Her school workload was getting heavier, though more interesting, too. She had been feeling guilty for not working more in the shop. Lao Zhao and his wife helped, but her father needed more hands.

"Ba, I agree with you. Let's sell the store."

***

The winter of 1951 was unusually cold. Mr. Liu was sick. He coughed constantly, and blood came out when he coughed.

"Send a telegram to Xi-Dan. Ask him to come home; I have things to tell him." He instructed Xiaojun one day.

Xi-Dan rushed home. After a quick hello and finding his father in better health than he'd expected, he went to the West House and stayed there with his wife Peifang and son Tiger.

Mr. Liu drifted in and out of sleep.

"Where's your brother?" He asked when he was awake.

"He said he'd be right back," Xiaojun wiped his forehead and sides of his mouth with a moist towel.

Mr. Liu slipped into unconsciousness, then woke again. He looked around the room. Xia was burying her head in a book next to the kang. Xiaojun was sewing a button onto a shirt. She attended to him as soon as he awoke. There'd still been no sign of Xi-Dan.

Mr. Liu sighed heavily.

"Tell Xi-Dan I've left a large amount of money in the space under the stove in the East House where your big brother used to live. It should be plenty to cover his schooling, the living expenses for Peifang, Tiger, and you two, and for Lao Zhao and his wife to continue caring for the house for several years."

Xiaojun remembered seeing Mr. Liu and Lao Zhao lifting some heavy bricks under the main cooking stove in the North House, the main house they lived with her father. "It needs to be cleaned," he'd explained to her at the time.

So, all stoves must have been a hiding place, Xiaojun thought.

"Ba. Don't say such things. You'll get better soon!" Xiaojun protested, her voice shaking.

"Junjun, I hope so. But I've made some plans." He coughed another heavy cough and spit out the blood onto the towel Xiaojun was holding.

Mr. Liu extended his hands to Xiaojun and Xia.

"Junjun and Xiaxia, I asked your Sanyi to safeguard 200 Da-Yang coins in case you two need extra money," he said with some effort. One Da-Yang was a round-shaped walnut-sized metal coin. They were long-lasting because of their metal materials and could be exchanged at the bank for paper currency.

"I hope you two stay in this house and watch Tiger grow up. He's our family bloodline," Mr. Liu continued.

"Ba," Xiaojun couldn't find the right words. This seemed so final and sad.

"I know. I'm not asking you to promise me."

"Ba, you'll get better soon. Don't say such terrible things." She looked at Xia's frightened face, her eyes wide open as if trying to escape the room. "Xia, go get Xi-Dan."

Xia flew out of the room.

"Junjun. I count on you to take care of Xiaxia."

"Ba, Xi-Dan and Peifang can do that too."

"But promise me you'll look after Xiaxia."

"I promise."

Xia slowly slid back into the room and quickly closed the door behind her. "He said he'll come right over once Tiger goes to sleep." She said it in a shameful voice, as if her words would cause trouble.

"Come here," Mr. Liu clenched Xiaojun's and Xia's hands. "Junjun and Xiaxia, I want you to hear me. Find your brother Xi-Chang no matter what. Tell him..." he coughed violently and let go of their hands. Xiaojun quickly rinsed the towel and padded the sides of his mouth.

"Tell him I saved enough money for him and his future family. The money is with the rest of the family treasure that I buried…"

Xiaojun waited. But Mr. Liu didn't continue. He closed his eyes as if saying, "I need to sleep now."

Xiaojun and Xia sat by the kang for a long time.

"It's late." Xiaojun said and got up. She put her hand under Mr. Liu's nose and could feel his exhales. "Ba is sleeping. He may get better tomorrow. You go to bed."

"Aren't you going too?" asked Xia.

"No, I'll stay with Ba."

The next morning, Xiaojun was awoken by a rooster's crowing. She was upset she hadn't stayed awake all night like she'd intended to. She hurried to her father and pushed him. But his body was cold and rigid, as if the central pillar of their home fell down from the roof.

6

HOME NO MORE

Xiaojun was filled with grief. In the span of just a few short years, she had lost her sister-in-law and both her parents. No one knew where her big brother was. The house was empty, depressing, and full of memories. But that wasn't all.

After Xiaojun told Xi-Dan about the money their father left them, Xi-Dan and Peifang dug up the stove in the East House. They found a sealed earthen jar with stacks of paper currency and metal coins. They also dug up the stoves in the other rooms but found only a few pieces of jewelry that had belonged to their mom.

"Are you telling the truth that Baba left money for Xi-Chang, too, but he didn't tell where it was?" Peifang questioned Xiaojun with sharp eyes.

Xiaojun couldn't believe what she was hearing. She couldn't stand anyone not trusting her. "Of course! How dare you even ask that?" *Who was she to accuse me? A brainless, heartless, lazy woman!*

"You were the only one present when he said this," Peifang followed.

Xi-Dan waved a hand at his wife as if to stop her. He turned to Xia with an encouraging expression. "No. Xia was there too."

"I, I, I can't remember. I don't remember what Ba said. I was afraid." Xia's voice showed plainly that even now she was still afraid.

Xi-Dan said, "I believe they're both telling the truth. Think about it—someone must have helped Ba do it, and it must be somewhere on this property, the only land we own. Digging up all these stoves took a lot of effort. Digging up other places won't be any easier. Where's Lao Zhao?"

Lao Zhao and his wife came.

"I only helped him to remove the stoves to clean them," Lao Zhao claimed. "I know nothing about hiding any family treasures."

"Hard to believe," Peifang snarled aggressively. "Did you put those stoves back in place after cleaning them?"

"Yes, I did. But I swear to Lao-Tian-Ye I know nothing about hiding anything." Lao Zhao's body shook, and his face turned red, as it always did whenever he had trouble making himself understood.

Lao Zhao's wife wiped her husband's forehead with a handkerchief. She gave Peifang a disgusted side eye and said gently, "Mr. Liu treated us well for decades. We believe in karma and wouldn't harm anyone."

The hidden family treasure was never found.

***

Xi-Dan went back to school after the Spring Festival. Peifang considered herself the head of the household because she was Xi-Dan's wife and the mother of the family's only heir, Tiger. Before Mr. Liu passed away, she did few household chores and spent most of her time taking care of Tiger. Now, she delegated all housework to Lao Zhao's wife.

One day at dinner, Xia said in a hesitant voice, "Umm, my feet hurt. I may need a pair of new shoes soon. These are becoming too small."

"Does Xiaojun's old pair fit you?" asked Peifang.

"I tried them, and they're too small, too," said Xia. She was as tall as Xiaojun now.

Peifang grew defensive. "Ask Lao Zhao's wife to make a pair!" She should be the person to make shoes and clothes. "Taking care of Tiger takes a lot of time and effort. I've got no time for anything else."

Xiaojun's face twisted in scorn. It was laughable. Peifang had just one child. Mrs. Liu had had four but had still found time to sew and make shoes.

Xia said in a low voice, "I did. She said it would take a while since she's been busy."

"Buy a new pair. I'm sure your brother would agree. Write to him to ask for money."

Xia looked desperate. That would take a long time, even if Xi-Dan wrote back.

Peifang stood up and went to get another pair of her shoes from the bedroom. She tossed them in front of Xia, "Try this old pair."

Xia put them on and was relieved. "They're tight, but better than my current ones."

Xiaojun said, "I'll make a pair for you."

Girls should know how to sew and make clothes, and she had watched her mom making such things. Jun had made a shirt for her Baba during the last Spring Festival—not because she'd been obliged to, but because she loved him. But she had yet to make shoes.

Xia was excited. "Jie, this pair can last for the winter. Make me a new pair for the warmer weather."

"It's about time you learn such things so you can serve your future husband and in-laws. Speaking of a husband, I've asked a matchmaker to find a suitor for you. You're almost seventeen now, a ripe age to get married."

"What?!" Xiaojun stared at Peifang in disbelief.

"You heard me. I was married at sixteen. Too bad Xia is still too young. But maybe in a couple of years, she'll get married too. The younger that you get married the better, because you can start your family life early and your children can grow when you're still young and have energy," Peifang said in a matter-of-fact voice.

But Xiaojun was furious. "Have you talked to my brother about this?"

"No need. He told me I should do whatever I think best."

"Did you know I told Ba I didn't want to get married too young?"

"I remember. That was then, and this is now. Ba is gone. You're under my care now."

"Your care? What care? You don't cook, you don't sew, and you don't do laundry. You do nothing in the house. But you have no trouble spending Ba's money. Now, less than one year after Ba's passing, you're already thinking about how to get rid of us. You'll never make me marry!"

Peifang didn't reply but wore a triumphant expression. She bent down and picked up Tiger. As if to drive her point home, she tickled Tiger under his chin, making him laugh loudly. Then she walked into the North House where Mr. Liu, Xiaojun and Xia used to live. Soon after his passing, Peifang had announced that the North

House was for the heads of the household, and she'd moved Xiaojun and Xia to the West House where she and Tiger used to live.

***

For several months, Xiaojun was busy after school. She consulted Lao Zhao's wife whenever she had shoemaking-related questions.

"I heard at the market that the government is taking over large houses." Lao Zhao's wife said worriedly.

"Will our house be targeted?" Xiaojun immediately asked, feeling quite concerned. Their house was one of the largest in the area.

"Who knows? Do you remember that man you used to get merchandise from for your Ba? I heard they kicked him out of his house recently."

"Where does he live now?" asked Xiaojun.

"No one knows. They called him a capitalist because he ran a shop. All capitalists must move out of their homes."

"Phew. It's a good thing Ba sold his shop. So maybe only the capitalists' homes are in danger?"

"Let's hope so. Here, you need to wrap up this edge before threading the laces through. You'll need to redo this. There's no way around it—if you don't, the shoe won't hold."

Xiaojun sighed. Another redo. It was much easier to watch her mom do it than to do it herself.

By the time spring arrived, Xiaojun had finished the new shoes for Xia. Seeing Xia's delightful face, Xiaojun felt pride and a strong sense of self-confidence. *I knew how to make clothes and now I know how to make shoes. I can always ask and learn if I don't know something.*

One summer day, two men visited right when they were about to have dinner.

"Sorry to delay your dinner," one of them said. "We're from the city government office. We heard Mr. Liu has passed away—our condolences."

The other man said, "We need to talk to the new head of the household."

This alarmed everyone, and they each looked around the room, dead silent.

Peifang's face was bright red. She opened her mouth, but nothing came out. She bent down, picked up Tiger, and held him to her chest tightly. When the men looked at her, she turned her face away and couldn't look the men in the eye.

Xiaojun sneered silently. *What a spineless coward.* She stepped forward and said,

"Thank you. My brother is out of town. Is there something we can help you with?"

"We understand your family is in possession of a large house that's being underutilized. Our office is expanding, and we'd like to use your house. We'll pay a reasonable rent."

Xiaojun looked at them carefully. They were dressed in decent clothes, like most educated people, and seemed like businessmen. There was no malice in their expressions. Xiaojun's experience of dealing with businesspeople told her these two men were trustworthy.

Xiaojun looked at Peifang, who was staring at the ground in front of her. She looked at Lao Zhao and his wife, who were watching with worry. She sensed Xia was hiding behind her.

Xiaojun cleared her throat and said, "This is big news. We need to let my brother know. Before I can write to him, can you provide written documentation of what your office plans to offer so I can pass those on to him?"

The men looked at Xiaojun with appreciation. "Very well. We'll bring a document by tomorrow."

Xi-Dan rushed home within two days of receiving the telegram from Xiaojun.

After reading the document carefully, he said, "This is a good idea. The house is indeed underutilized. It's better for it to be rented by a government office than be taken away, like what's happened to capitalists and landlords."

Xiaojun agreed. She had been worried about the house for some time now. She observed, "But we'll have to find a smaller place to live. The renters' money might help, along with what Ba left us."

"We can let Lao Zhao and his wife find their place." Peifang chipped in.

"What? They've been in the family ever since I was born," Xiaojun protested.

"Since I was born, too," Xi-Dan added.

"There was a lot of housework back then. But once you two get married and Tiger gets bigger..." Peifang trailed off.

Xiaojun looked at Peifang with disgust. "I've told you I'm not getting married!"

Xi-Dan looked at Peifang, then Xiaojun. "It's not a bad idea to get married. You're what, 18 now? Almost an old maid already. This might be a good time to find a husband and move into his home."

Xiaojun's face turned red and her eyes filled with fire. *He overestimated my age!* She shouted at Xi-Dan, "I cannot believe you said that! I thought you were an educated person. I'm not someone you can just get rid of. Plus, what about Xia?"

"Xia can live with me and take care of Tiger. After a few years, she'll marry, too," Peifang suggested.

"No!" Xia said in a loud voice she'd never used before.

Xi-Dan sighed. He wasn't fond of dealing with business or family affairs and just wanted this to be resolved as soon as possible.

He turned to his sister and asked her, "Xiaojun, what do you want?"

Xiaojun paused for a moment, and said, "Ba said he left enough money for you, Peifang, Tiger, and the two of us for years to come. He wanted Xia and I to live in the house to watch Tiger grow up. If you want to rent out the house, it's your decision. But Xia and I need a place to live, and money. We will not be married off. We count on you to share the money for our living expenses."

Peifang sneered. Xi-Dan was silent, contemplating.

"Also, Ba did not say we should get rid of Lao Zhao and his wife," Xiaojun continued. "If they need to find a place, we should provide some money to support them."

Peifang wanted to say something, but Xi-Dan waved a hand and stopped her.

"Alright. Here's my decision. We'll rent the house to the government. Each month, Peifang will collect money from them. She'll also give you two a certain amount of money for your living expenses. It seems you and Xia should find a place to live, and I'll find somewhere for Peifang and Tiger. I'll take care of Lao Zhao and his wife; you don't have to worry about them."

"You remember Peifang can't read or count, right?" Xiaojun said scornfully.

Peifang's face turned purple. She almost hit Xiaojun with her fist. "I can count money!"

Xia stepped forward. "I'll go with Peifang to collect the rent money."

Xi-Dan nodded. "Then it's all set. I'll put Peifang and Xia's names down on the paper under 'collectors.'"

***

Fall, 1952. Xiaojun, 17, and Xia, 14, stood in front of a door at the end of an extensive building comprising many classrooms. Several spider webs filled with desiccated dead bugs blocked the door, which had chipped paint. The small glass window above the door was as dirty as it could be.

The middle-aged school principal opened the dusty lock and pushed the door open. A disgusting smell escaped. Xia covered her mouth with her hand. Right at that moment, a mouse rushed out of the door. Xiaojun jumped. "Ah!"

The principal looked at them with sympathy. "You two can use this room. It's a storage room. I'll have the furniture removed. We can put two beds here."

He looked at the room, then the girls, and added, "We won't charge you any rent. Your father was a great man."

What a tremendous relief for Xiaojun and Xia. The amount of money they got from Xi-Dan and Peifang was barely enough to cover food and materials for making clothes and shoes.

The narrow room had just enough space to put two single beds on either wall with a narrow path between them. It was a long room, however, so there would be room to put a desk, a washbowl stand, and some luggage, though the girls had little. Xiaojun and Xia had only brought their clothes, shoes, some bedding, and school items, leaving all their other belongings in storage at home.

7

FIRST LOVE

Life at school was quiet and time passed quickly. 1953 came. One year had come and gone since they had lived in the schoolroom, they now called home.

Laundry was Xia's responsibility. Hand-scrubbing clothes in cold water, especially in winter, was grueling work, but Xia did it diligently, without complaining. Someone had to do it, and Xia knew her sister was already doing so much. As long as Xia could still find time to read novels and take part in athletic activities, especially playing basketball, she was content.

Xiaojun spent her spare time sewing clothes, making shoes, cooking, and cleaning their room. She dedicated some of her time to tutoring Xia, too. Not inclined toward sports, the literary arts, or any pursuits that were purely for enjoyment, Xiaojun focused on things she considered being purposeful. Although she wasn't sure where her education might lead, she knew if she did well, she could earn respect from both her teachers and her peers.

School was easy for Xiaojun, and she excelled in all her assignments and exams. She found a quiet place, the attic of a large classroom no one else knew about, and hid there for a couple of hours after school each day to finish all homework. She only needed to review her study materials once to engrave the information on her brain. If it was up to her, she'd move faster and finish school sooner, but she didn't want to leave Xia behind. She had been one grade higher than Xia throughout their school years.

As a co-ed school, about a third of the students were girls. Each grade had one class and students from all grades mingled and played with each other in sporting events and social activities.

On the first day of the new school year, a new student walked into Xiaojun's classroom.

The teacher introduced him to the class. "This is Yanshao. He and his mom moved to this area from a neighboring city."

The teacher turned to the young man. "You can sit with Xiaojun in the last row."

Yanshao was taller than the other students, so of course he'd have to sit in the last row like Xiaojun, who was the tallest among the girls and even taller than some boys. Yanshao's slightly curly hair set him apart from other students, who all had straight black hair. A small lock of hair dangled over his forehead. He had a high nose bridge, rounded cheeks, and smooth jawlines. He had double eyelids too, like Xiaojun, and his eyes were also like Xiaojun's, in the shape of a half-cherry, especially when he smiled. It was hard not to stare at him—he seemed to be the very definition of handsome.

As Yanshao walked to his seat, all the students' eyes followed him.

He nodded at Xiaojun with a smile and sat down neatly.

Xiaojun's heart skipped a beat, but she pretended to be her normal self, giving him a polite nod, and turning her face back toward the front of the classroom. She noticed all the girls were still staring at Yanshao, and some wore clearly envious expressions when they glanced at her next to him.

School life had suddenly become a lot more interesting. Xiaojun looked forward to starting each school day. Even Xia didn't need to be pushed awake in the morning. Her laundry frequency increased too and Xiaojun had to remind her, "You're going to rub holes into the clothes if you wash them too often." "But I want to look neat and clean," Xia replied.

In the past, Xiaojun hadn't enjoyed recess or physical education classes. But now she looked forward to them, because she'd be able to watch Yanshao in different settings outside the classroom. Whenever she could, she would snatch a peek at Yanshao. If she couldn't find him right away, she'd keep looking around until he jumped into view. She quickly learned that his good manners matched his good looks—he never said a bad word or lost his temper. He seemed much more mature than the oldest student. And he was athletic.

The two basketball teams fought to get Yanshao to join. Xia excitedly told Xiaojun that he'd joined her team. "Boy, he was so good at shooting baskets, and he moves so fast." Xia couldn't hide her high opinion of him. She reported to Xiaojun daily about their basketball practices or matches, and she mentioned his name constantly.

As more proof of his athleticism, in the first sports competition of the year, Yanshao won first place in the long jump, 100-meter run, and shot put.

More and more girls found excuses to approach him whenever they could.

One girl rushed to Xiaojun's side of the table as soon as class had ended. "Hi! Yanshao! Since you're so good at answering all the questions from the teacher, could you tutor me?"

Xiaojun rolled her eyes. It was as if she, Xiaojun, didn't exist, even though she was right under the girl's nose and she was also one who raised her hand and answered all the questions.

A tall girl said to Yanshao before class was to start, "I'm hoping to join the basketball team. Can you help me practice after school?"

Xiaojun rolled her eyes again. According to Xia, her team had tried to recruit this tall girl last year, hoping her height could be a boon for the team, but she'd declined.

In each of these instances, Yanshao would happily oblige.

Like a fly on a wall, Xiaojun observed these interactions with distaste.

The entire school is in love with him. Correction: Almost every girl is in love with him. But not me. He's attractive. But he pays attention to every girl, and I won't stand for that, Xiaojun reminded herself. She was glad she hadn't thrown herself at him like all the other girls did.

By the end of the first semester, Yanshao's outstanding performance in all subjects had earned him recognition as one of the top two students. The other student was Xiaojun. Yanshao smiled brightly at Xiaojun when they walked back to their seats after receiving their awards. Xiaojun politely nodded to him and sat down, facing forward.

Yanshao leaned over slightly and whispered in her ear, "I'd like to talk with you after school."

Without turning her head, Xiaojun said, "Okay." Her heart leaped. But no one could tell—she concealed it well.

That afternoon, Yanshao didn't show up to basketball practice. Instead, he and Xiaojun went to a quiet place by the far end of the playground where a huge old tree stood.

"I heard from Xia your parents passed away," he began, sympathy in his voice.

"Yes," said Xiaojun. *People in the school know that.*

"I never met my dad. He left before I was born," he admitted, his hands playing with a leaf.

Xiaojun became intrigued. She knew nothing about his background. She'd overheard other girls talking about how they were dying to know more about him, but he was tight-lipped and never answered questions when asked.

Xiaojun carefully chose her words. "So, your mom raised you alone?"

"Yes. She worked as a housekeeper for as long as I can remember. Last year, her Ma, my Lao Lao (Chinese for grandma), was sick and asked us to move back to help."

Xiaojun said nothing but her dark eyes asked, *Why are you telling me this?*

He looked at her with an awkward smile and said, "I don't know why I told you that. I haven't told anyone about it."

He lowered his head for a moment, then looked up at her again. "I like you and want to be your friend. You're different from all the other girls."

Xiaojun's words popped up without a filter. "You're friendly with all the other girls."

"I try. Being a housekeeper's son, you learn quickly that being friendly is the key to having a peaceful life, and to making your mom proud and less worried."

"To be fair, you're friendly with me too," Xiaojun said, then followed that with, "I believe I'm friendly with you as well."

"Yes, but…" He paused, trying to find the right words, "Yes, you're friendly and polite. But you're also distant. You might be the only girl who never showed eagerness to talk with me."

Xiaojun raised one of her eyebrows and said slowly, "So, you want every girl to talk with you, and eagerly."

"No, no, that's not what I meant. It didn't come out right." He wiped his forehead with one hand and pushed the lock of curly hair upward.

Xiaojun looked at him squarely in the face, one eyebrow raised again as if asking, *Then, what did you mean?*

Yanshao swallowed. "What I meant is, umm, I find you much more mature than the rest. You have common sense and don't say or do shallow things. You're smart and an excellent student. And you remind me of my mom. You're strong to raise yourself and your baby sister. Plus, you have great manners, and, and… you're beautiful." He seemed relieved once the last word had come out.

Xiaojun had butterflies in her stomach. She opened her mouth to say something. Just then, a girl running on the track said from a distance, "Hi, Yanshao!"

"Hi," Yanshao waved back, and quickly faced Xiaojun. "You were saying?"

Xiaojun closed her mouth. The butterflies disappeared. After a moment's pause, she said in a matter-of-fact tone,

"I'm older than all the other students, and my sister and I are the only ones living in a schoolroom. Of course, I'm more mature and different from them."

"I wish I could help you and Xia. It must be hard."

"I appreciate your kind thoughts. We're managing. Plus, it's obvious you're pretty busy already, and here comes your reading buddy." She glanced at a girl walking in their direction, books in her arms.

Yanshao's face turned red. He wiped his forehead. "I'm sorry to give you the wrong impression. I should be more careful when I interact with other girls."

Xiaojun walked away. *What a playboy.*

In the months following that meeting, Xiaojun noticed Yanshao was watching her expressions closely. He seemed to try to make sure whatever he did wasn't offending her. She also kept hearing complaints from other girls.

"Yanshao canceled our regular reading meetings. I don't know what's up with him—it can't possibly be that his mom is sick that often," one girl said.

"'It's definitely strange—he said he couldn't help me with math after school," another girl piped up.

Even Xia commented about Yanshao, "He stayed only for basketball practice, then rushed home afterward. He used to stick around and shoot baskets with us."

Xiaojun was curious if this had to do with their talk. She wanted to believe so, but she also wanted to be cautious. Plus, what if something had indeed happened at his home?

"Is your mom all right?" Xiaojun asked in a whisper one day, before class had begun.

"She had a cold, but she's fine now," Yanshao whispered back. He was both surprised and delighted by the question.

"That's good." Xiaojun sat down without looking at him.

"Actually, could you help me with the math problem we learned this morning? I'm having trouble understanding it," Yanshao whispered, also not looking at her.

Xiaojun turned her head toward him to make sure she'd heard right. *He's asking me for help? On math?*

Yanshao turned to her and gave her an earnest look. She nodded without saying a word. Sitting in the last row, few of their classmates could hear or see them.

8

SCARE

Xiaojun and Yanshao met once a week for schoolwork. Yanshao claimed he needed help, and he made this even more clear during class by asking questions to show he was uncertain about the concepts. That made it more legitimate for him to stay after class at their desk so Xiaojun could go through the materials with him, usually under the jealous gaze of other girls.

Xiaojun found her understanding improved after she explained the materials to him. She thought he was extremely smart—he'd grasp the ideas and repeat them back in his own words. She didn't think he actually needed any help and suspected it was just an excuse to spend time with her. But if so, she didn't care. She enjoyed the time they spent together, and she was secretly delighted that she seemed to be the only person he spent time with after school. He rushed home as soon as all school-related obligations were finished. He politely declined requests from anyone else.

When schoolwork was done, the two of them randomly talked a little about this or that.

"I have to deliver some finished clothes to customers today," he said one day. "My mom sews to earn money," he explained.

"How is your Lao Lao?"

"She's fine. Her eyes got bad, and she couldn't sew anymore. So, my mom took over the orders from her customers. It's good income."

"It must be. You're lucky to have money to buy sports shoes. Xia has been asking for a long time for a pair of shoes for basketball. I've finally saved enough for her."

"Do you need any help? I could lend you my allowance."

Xiaojun gave him a look that made him immediately regret what he'd said.

"We can manage. Plus," she paused and said, "people often have expectations for payback when they offer help."

Yanshao blushed, rambling, "Oh. I know you can handle it. I just wanted you to know in case you needed money. Well... I should go home now."

One afternoon, Xiaojun came back home from studying in her hiding place. She found the door half open and heard moaning. Quickly stepping in, she saw Xia lying in bed crying with her eyes closed and face red. Her body was curved like a shrimp and her hands were pressed against her stomach. Yanshao was sitting next to her with a damp towel, dabbing her forehead.

Yanshao got to his feet as soon as Xiaojun entered and said, "We need to get her to the hospital. She felt this pain before we started practice, and then it got worse."

Xiaojun put her hand on Xia's forehead—it was burning hot. This differed from the monthly episodes that would land Xia in bed for at least a day.

Xiaojun sat on the edge of the bed and examined Xia's face, hands, neck, and under her eyelids. "What could this be? Was it bad food? Was it the cold water you used for laundry yesterday? But you always use cold water."

Xia's crying became screaming. It was obvious the pain was unbearable.

"Show me where it hurts," asked Xiaojun.

Xia screamed louder. She pointed to the right side of her lower abdomen.

Xiaojun did a quick mental check of the money they had. It would barely cover their living expenses for this month, and who knew how much the treatment might cost?

Yanshao saw her hesitation. "We should take her to the hospital. Something's seriously wrong. We'll worry about money later."

Xiaojun looked at him, and saw a mix of concern, eagerness, and determination in his eyes.

She turned to Xia, "Stand up. Can you walk?"

Xia struggled to sit up. The two of them held each of her arms and pulled her to her feet. She immediately bent down to hold her stomach.

Yanshao said hurriedly, "she can't walk. I'll borrow a cart from the school."

A few minutes later, Yanshao and Xiaojun put Xia on a two-wheeled flatbed cart that was normally used to carry goods and, occasionally, people. Xiaojun walked alongside and held Xia, and Yanshao pulled with great effort. They arrived at the hospital in 30 minutes.

The doctor examined Xia and turned to Xiaojun and Yanshao. "It's appendicitis. It's good you got her here in time. We need to operate on her immediately."

Xiaojun was shocked. "Operation? What kind? Will she be alright?" Operations always sounded fatal. From what she heard, people would often die, either during or after the operation.

The doctor answered, "Her appendix is inflamed and is causing a problem. It's a common operation. She should recover soon."

Xiaojun thought it couldn't be that simple. "But are there any risks with the operation?"

The doctor said, "Yes, there are potential risks, including infection, which may cause death. But if we don't operate, she will die."

The words "death" and "die" made Xiaojun's face white and her body tremble. Her mind was screaming, "No! No!" and her world began turning around her. She couldn't lose another family member.

Yanshao caught her in time and held her in his arms.

"Doctor, could you save her, please?" Xiaojun heard the sob in her voice.

"Yes, we'll do our best. Here's the paperwork you need to sign. It says you're the family of the patient and you allow us to operate on your sister." The doctor passed a piece of paper.

With a shaky hand, Xiaojun signed the paper.

In the waiting room, Xiaojun couldn't sit still. She paced back and forth, worst-case scenarios running through her head. She was in her own world, oblivious to what was going on around her.

Yanshao left the hospital briefly and returned with steamed buns. He quietly watched Xiaojun for a few minutes, then walked over to her and led her to a chair. "You must be hungry. I've brought some food from home."

Xiaojun came back to reality. She looked at Yanshao and couldn't control her tears anymore.

What if he hadn't been there to convince her to bring Xia to the hospital? What if he hadn't been there to pull the cart?

She stared at him and realized he was someone who had shared the load that had, for so many years now, rested on her shoulders alone. She grabbed his hands and sobbed uncontrollably. He held her hands quietly.

A nurse came and said, "You two can visit your sister now."

The next day, Xiaojun and Yanshao brought Xia home. They had lunch together in Xiaojun and Xia's room. It was the first of many meals they had together. Even Xia—a happy, bighearted, carefree girl—could sense that sharing these meals meant the trio was a family now. She was delighted to see Yanshao more frequently and in this capacity, too. She was happy for her sister, who now smiled often.

9

PROSPECTS

Middle school graduation day was fast approaching. For many of the students, this would be the end of their formal education. For a few, further studies awaited.

One afternoon, after finishing studying in the hiding place in the attic they now shared, Yanshao said to Xiaojun, "My mom is getting old. Her eyes have problems, and her hands can't hold the needles steadily. Her fingers are often bleeding. I don't want to add to her burden by going all the way to college. I want to find a job. But my mom insists I should continue. You know I'd do anything for her to make her happy. So, I might go to a vocational school."

Starting in 1953, the Chinese Communist Party established a five-year plan every five years to chart out its social and economic development initiatives. 1956 was the year the country was in the middle of its first five-year plan. A more educated workforce was in high demand for many positions. In response to this need, policymakers established vocational schools as an alternative to colleges. These schools prepared students to start certain jobs immediately after three years of study. To attract students, vocational schools covered room and board and tuition, as well as a small monthly allowance.

In contrast, colleges remained expensive and typically required four to five years to finish. Students or their families covered the costs of tuition, room and board, and living expenses, though there were a limited number of scholarships for academically or athletically outstanding candidates. To enter college, one needed to spend three more years in high school.

"You could apply for college scholarships. You have the double advantage of being advanced in both academics and sports," said Xiaojun.

"Is that what you want? To go to college?" asked Yanshao.

"College is more prestigious and would earn more respect. But I can't afford it without a scholarship." Xiaojun sighed.

"You should apply for one because you've consistently been a straight-A student all these years. If anyone can get it, it would be you."

"For you, it's certain. Besides the double advantage, you have another advantage: You're a male. Many people still suppose girls don't need to go to school. As you can tell, the teachers and students treat you and me differently even though we're both straight-A students."

Yanshao was silent. He had noticed this too and was furious Xiaojun didn't get the recognition she deserved.

"And my name on the application form will give away my gender," Xiaojun said glumly.

They were both quiet. Then they looked at each other as they both realized something.

"What if..." Yanshao started.

"Yeah, what if I change my name so people won't be able to tell my gender when they read my application?" Xiaojun followed.

"Even better, what if they thought you were a male when they saw your name?" Yanshao asked excitedly.

Xiaojun gave an appreciative look at Yanshao. That would be great! She was tired of her name, so feminine and weak—the Little Pretty Girl, as if she was still little, and she had no qualities except being pretty. It had served its purpose for her parents. She'd love to have a new identity with a new name.

"I want to drop 'Xiao' in the name. I'm not little anymore," Xiaojun reasoned. "But if there's a way to keep part of the name from my parents, that would be ideal."

"Let's see. If we change 'Jun' to a different character of the same sound, you'd still be able to honor your parents."

They sounded out "Jun" in four intonations. Yanshao got out a dictionary.

"Here! How about this word: Jun, a gentleman, someone with an excellent education and polite manner, someone who earns respect from society."

"Perfect!" Xiaojun exclaimed delightedly.

She approached the school office and changed her name in all paperwork, transcripts, and her student profile:

Liu Xiaojun 刘小俊 → Liu Jun 刘君

10

MAKING ENDS MEET

What if I don't get a scholarship for college after three years of high school?

Jun woke up in the middle of the night, panting.

She had calculated the potential costs of going to high school for both her and Xia. So far, the spending money came from Peifang as a monthly allowance. The two of them were at the mercy of Xi-Dan and Peifang.

On Sunday, Jun took Xia to visit Peifang and Tiger. It had been Xia to retrieve the money. She was friendly with Peifang and enjoyed seeing Tiger. Jun couldn't stand seeing Peifang's face as she handed out Ba's money.

Peifang and Tiger lived in a small rental house on the edge of the city. Six-year-old Tiger was healthy and happy. Peifang had done a great job raising him by herself.

Jun felt guilty for not seeing Tiger much. She remembered what her father asked her before dying: "I hope you two stay in this house and watch Tiger grow up." Letting out a heavy sigh, Jun murmured to herself, *Ba, you couldn't have known how things would change.*

"Glad you two are back to see Tiger. Since your brother divorced me and left Tiger with me to raise, we're moving back to live with my parents soon," Peifang disclosed sadly.

"What?" Jun and Xia exclaimed at the same time.

"When did this happen?" Jun asked.

"He came home last month to complete the paperwork." Peifang wiped her eyes.

"So that's what it was about?" Xia suddenly said, a strange expression on her face.

"You knew about this?" Jun turned to face Xia.

"Well, he came to see us and you were with Yanshao somewhere, so he took me to the market. We had some candies and a delightful meal. Umm, I didn't tell you because I thought you'd be upset about it." Xia's face was full of guilt.

Jun was furious. *How could he not say hi to me after not seeing me for such a long time? What gave him the right to waste precious money? How could he divorce his wife? How could he abandon his son, who might be the only bloodline carrier of the family?*

"What about the money Ba left for the household? For the five of us?" Jun asked Peifang.

"Ask your brother. I don't know how much is left. He always only told me to pass a certain amount to you girls, and he'd leave some for Tiger and me to use."

"Thank goodness, at least we still have the monthly rent," Jun murmured.

"Umm, well. I was going to tell you about that..." Xia's sheepish voice told Xiaojun this couldn't be good news.

"Xi-Dan said, umm, that it was too much trouble to keep up the repairs, and umm, also, the government has been holding the rent and debating what to do, given our family class." Xia spilled out the words painfully, as if she had a toothache.

Their family class was "Rich People" because they owned an enormous property.

"And?" Jun stared at Xia intensely.

"And, umm, he fixed a deal. He said it's a good deal with the government. He sold the house." Xia exhaled once the last word was out.

"What? Why didn't he discuss this with us before selling the house? And what about those treasures Ba buried somewhere? We haven't found them and now we'll never find them!" Jun was beyond furious, her lips trembling.

Xia and Peifang stood there silently, expressionless.

"I'll write to him," Jun squeezed the words out of her lips.

"Umm, well, he gave me a new address last month," Xia said in a low voice.

"And you didn't tell me? Where is he now?" Jun's stare made Xia want to find a hole in the ground to escape to.

Peifang said, "He said he had finished his teacher's training school and started working as a teacher in Hebei province."

"Hebei Province? Which city? How far is it from here?" Jun asked.

Peifang shook her head as if to say, "What difference does it make?"

***

Jun and Xia left Peifang and Tiger. Part of Jun pitied Peifang for the first time. After all, she was raising a boy for the family.

Jun was not hopeful that she and Xia could get much money from Xi-Dan, even though Xia had said he'd promised to send them money monthly from the proceeds of the sale of their house.

Wait, Ba told us about the secret money he put away at Sanyi's in case we needed it.

Jun and Xia had seen Sanyi only once after their father passed away. She had become widowed and lived with her adult son in the countryside. Their class was "Peasant" because they didn't own land or houses.

"We've got to be careful and not attract attention. Some people may report to the authorities we interacted with Rich People," Sanyi whispered and rushed to give Jun a bag, and said, "Here's the money your Ba left for you. Now run away before people see you two."

Once back in their room, Jun opened the bag and counted. It was 185 Da-Yang, with 15 missing from what Ba told her.

"You heard Ba said it was 200, right?" She asked Xia to be sure.

"Yes, 200," Xia confirmed angrily. "How could Sanyi do this to us? That's a lot of money!"

"We should have checked the money in front of her. We were in such a hurry. She made us scared, like we needed to run. Now I want to know if she'd admit to stealing the money if we confronted her."

"We should go back to ask her. It's a lot of money." Xia was furious.

Two weeks later, they visited Sanyi again.

White banners with black-inked characters adorned the door of Sanyi's house. The girls looked at each other and held each other's hands. They knew too well what it meant.

When Sanyi opened the door and saw them, she collapsed on the floor. She kneeled facing south and repeatedly knocked her forehead on the floor with a loud sound. She rambled non-stop.

"I didn't mean to touch the money. I didn't! But we had no food. We were starving. Lao-Tian-Ye. Please hear me! You know I resisted. I tried hard not to touch the money. But my boy, he was starving. He was dying. Lao-Tian-Ye! I've heard you now, I've heard you! It's karma. You took my boy away. Please forgive me, please! Lao-Tian-Ye!"

A neighbor came by just then with some food for Sanyi. She pulled the girls aside and told them Sanyi's son had died last week. "He was walking next to a wall he passed by every day, and it collapsed on him with no warning. He never woke up."

11

FAR AWAY

Jun and Xia left Sanyi's place with heavy hearts. They took the rest of the Da-Yang to the bank to exchange it for paper currency.

"Haven't seen these for a while. Family treasure?" The guy behind the counter asked.

"Yeah. My father left them for us."

"They aren't worth much now. The government tried to collect them from circulation. I can give you the exchange, but you'll be disappointed," the guy said.

"How much could I get?" asked Jun.

He passed a few paper bills to her. "This is what it's worth now. The exchange rate has decreased and may continue to do so."

She counted and calculated. The money might last three months for the two of them, mainly for food and other necessities.

Even with Xi-Dan's unreliable charity from the house sale money, Jun couldn't imagine three more years of high school and then four years of college. She would have to find a good-paying job if she wanted to continue high school. What skills did she have? How much time would she have to study if she had to work? How much pay could she get? What chance would she have to receive a college scholarship? And even if she received a scholarship, would it be enough? And what about Xia? She needed money, too. She wore shoes out twice as fast as Jun did. Xia had been growing so fast that Xiaojun's old clothes didn't fit her anymore and she needed new clothes often.

What if I go to a vocational school? The school would cover my living expenses, and I could save some allowance to help Xia. She could go to high school and college. She's bright and deserves it. Plus, if I go to a vocational school, I might go with Yanshao.

***

Among the few choices presented by the recruiters, Jun and Yanshao focused on an engineering school in Hohhot, Inner Mongolia.

"Many places need electricity generated from water," a female recruiter from the vocational school said during a group meeting. "Training at engineering schools offers a strong chance for prestigious jobs. Our school is the top-ranking institution of this kind. Our funding is better than other schools, too," she added.

Jun raised her hand and asked, "Do you accept both girls and boys?"

"Oh, yes. About one-third of our student population is female. We consider boys and girls as equally capable. We just want good, ambitious students."

Yanshao remembered reading from somewhere that Inner Mongolia was in the grasslands. He asked, "Is the school on grassland? Do people ride horses and live in tents?"

The recruiter laughed. "Our school is in the capital city, and the city doesn't differ from Chifeng. The residents there are like people you see here, with a similar lifestyle and even similar food. Residents live in houses and sleep in the kang, like you do here. But in school, there are wooden beds in the student dorms. You need to travel quite a distance from the city to visit the grassland. But you will see it, and it's beautiful."

"Is the school far away from here?" Jun followed. She worried about seeing Xia. And Yanshao would need to visit his mom too.

"You'll take a daytime train ride from Chifeng to Beijing and an overnight train ride from Beijing to Hohhot. Once you get there, we'll pick you up from the train station," the recruiter said, using the future tense as if Jun had already decided. She continued, "Keep in mind, this school produces highly promising students for high-demand jobs."

"What kind of job titles will the students have when they enter the workforce?" Jun asked.

"They'll be civil engineers."

After the meeting, Jun and Yanshao discussed the merits of the school.

"This engineering school seems the most interesting one of all the ones we've learned about so far. And I'd like to be an engineer. It sounds so prestigious," Jun mused.

"I agree. I could see myself going there," Yanshao followed.

"Will you go? Will your mom let you?"

"My mom will let me go to any school. So I'm sure I can convince her."

"I've never left Chifeng in my life. Have you ever traveled that far?" asked Jun.

"Not that far, and only by buses. It will be fun to take a train, and an overnight train!" Yanshao sounded excited.

"I agree. It's so exciting." Jun could see herself on the train, although she didn't know what the inside of a train even looked like. She'd only seen trains while passing railroad crossings.

Yanshao examined the bright eyes on Jun's dreamy face, and said slowly, "We should go. It will be easier if we're together. We can help each other."

Jun stared back at him, flushed with thoughts and emotions. He had become such an important person in her life now. He gave her hope and support, making her life endurable and enjoyable. Whether or not she needed it, he cared for her. She couldn't imagine a life without him. Of course she wanted to go with him to the vocational school. She knew she had to leave her baby sister behind. But Xia had assured Jun if Yanshao could leave his mom to go to school far away, then Jun could leave her and let her grow and become independent. "I am 18 now. You started taking care both of us before this age," she reminded Jun.

"I agree. We can help each other. Let's go," Jun said firmly.

Part II

Hohhot, 1956–1962

12

BLUE CITY

Summer 1956. Jun and Yanshao got off the train and stepped into the open square in front of Hohhot Train Station. Surrounded by several scattered one-story buildings, the square felt open and expansive. The sky seemed within reach, visible with no need to look up, seamlessly connected to a wide paved road. And what a deep blue the sky was! A color neither of them had seen in their hometown. The dry air quickly whisked away the sweat on her face and neck, built up from sitting on the hot train and carrying two large pieces of luggage.

"It feels so good. I like it here already," Jun smiled at Yanshao. She set down her bags and looked around again, absorbing a sense of hope and freedom.

"I agree," Yanshao nodded, setting down his own bags next to hers.

It was still early in the morning, and the square was quiet, with only a few people. So was the road ahead of it.

A young man with a pair of glasses walked toward them. "Are you new students at the vocational school?"

"Yes, we are. This is Liu Jun, and I'm Ge Yanshao." Yanshao extended a hand but was unsure if a handshake was a norm here or not.

"Nice to meet you. I'm Ouyang. Come and meet another new student. I'll take you three to campus." Ouyang didn't shake Yanshao's hand. He waved hello, then led them to a cart not far away.

The cart's front looked like a bike, but the back was a boxy unit on four wheels with two benches that could seat six skinny people.

A boyish man was already on the back bench, and two bags occupied part of the bench. He watched the three of them approaching the cart and stared at Jun's face intensely.

Jun and Yanshao said a quick hi to the man and sat on the front bench after loading their luggage.

"It'll take about thirty or thirty-five minutes because the school is on the south side—the opposite of the train station. So, hold on. Here we go." Ouyang got on the rider's seat, pushed the ground with one leg, and started pedaling and turning the cart toward the road.

The road was lined with a few one-story buildings on either side that gradually gave way to farm fields. Jun recognized corn and potato crops. Far off in the distance on all three sides were dark gray mountains. Jun turned around and saw mountains behind them, too, rising not far beyond the train station.

Jun's eyes met the boyish man's gaze.

"Hi, I'm Jun," she said, wanting to be polite.

Yanshao turned around, too, and said, "And I'm Yanshao. What's your name?"

The man's Adam's apple jumped a few times. He cleared his throat and said, "Wu Dazhi. I'm Wu Dazhi." His eyes flicked away from Jun's face and he looked like he'd been caught stealing.

"We're from Chifeng. Where are you from, Dazhi?" Yanshao inquired.

"Taiyuan." His accent was more pronounced now. As if not knowing what to say next, he lowered his eyes.

Yanshao nodded with a smile. He turned around and said, "Hi, Ouyang. Do you know how many new students are coming this year?"

Ouyang's breathing steadied as the cart glided smoothly along the paved road. "I believe 30. We're supposed to pick up about 20 from the train station today. A few will come by bus, and we have people picking them up there, too. A few are local and they'll make their own way to campus."

"How long have you been at the school?" Yanshao asked.

"This is my second year. My cohort was the first. We started with 30 but now we have 29 students. Next year, you'll be picking up the new students." Ouyang turned around and smiled at Yanshao.

Jun asked, "Ouyang, are those corn and potatoes? Where's the high grassland?"

Ouyang turned and said, "They are. The mountain ranges create a unique environment around Hohhot. It supports agriculture with typical crops for the northern regions. But Inner Mongolia is vast, and much of it is dominated by expansive high grasslands."

"The sky is so blue!" Jun gushed.

"Yup, and that's why the city's nickname is Blue City," said Ouyang.

"Is it always this blue?" asked Jun.

"Pretty much. We get rain and snow, but they're rare. Clouds never stay for very long," promised Ouyang.

"Those mountains, they look grayish, but not quite gray," said Jun.

"No, they're not gray. They're blue, of course, a different blue than the sky. They're called the Blue Mountains. That's another reason Hohhot's nickname is Blue City, because the Blue Mountains surround it."

How interesting. Chifeng is red mountains, and here they have blue mountains. Jun made a mental note.

Thirty minutes later, Ouyang steered the cart to a gate with two metal panels, flanked by school banners on the side pillars—one in Chinese and the other in Mongolian. A small room adjoined the gate. Walls as tall as the height of a person surrounded the campus.

"Hi, Mr. Li!" Ouyang called out, waving.

An older man came out of the small room, pushed one gate panel to the side, and gestured to Ouyang to go through.

"Thank you!" Ouyang shouted.

"There's a guard for the campus?" Yanshao was amazed.

"Yes. This is the only gate to campus. The attendants guard the gate 24 hours a day. Students can't leave during the night, and outsiders need to get permission to enter. You'd better become good friends with the attendants."

Inside the gate, two rows of young poplars lined the road. Tall and slender, their clean trunks stretched upward, with branches sprouting around shoulder height. Together, they formed a fence-like barrier below and a leafy canopy above, casting shade over the road.

Jun recalled seeing many poplar-lined roads near the train station, although these trees here were noticeably younger.

Ouyang paused the cart in front of a group of four red-brick, two-story buildings. "This area is the academic quarter. These buildings have classrooms, laboratories, and a library. Each evening, all the rooms are locked."

Ouyang guided the cart down the road and into an open area behind the academic quarter.

Yanshao's eyes widened, blinking rapidly. "Wow!" He exclaimed with delight.

"Yes, we have a vast playground. I was just as amazed when I first saw it."

As if to prolong their delight, Ouyang circled the playground, giving the three newcomers a chance to take it all in.

The largest section featured areas for long jump, high jump, and other field activities, encircled by a 400-meter oval track. To the east lay four basketball courts next to a handful of badminton courts, while the west was dominated by a spacious soccer field. On the north side stood a two-story building.

"There's a canteen on the first floor of this building. You can find some entertainment facilities upstairs, like Ping-Pong tables, chess boards, newspapers, magazines, and a radio set."

Ouyang parked the cart between the canteen and a group of three red-brick, three-story buildings.

"These are the living quarters. Those two buildings are male dormitories, and this one is for girls. You can get hot water any time of the day from the room connected to the bathhouse. Gentlemen, I'm going to unload Jun's luggage, then yours. You can find the registration office in Academic Building 1. You'll be able to get your meal tickets, books, and other essentials there. Keep in mind, lunch is from noon to one o'clock."

13

SCHOOL FOR GROWNUPS

Jun and Yanshao transitioned into student life easily. They liked the food from the canteen, although they both craved hometown food. The coursework was manageable, and they both found social activities to pass the time.

The two-day annual sports competition came when fall started. There were no classes, and everyone was expected to take part. Some did one sport, while others—like Yanshao and Ouyang—did all eight.

Ouyang persuaded Jun to join the high jump competition and the ladies' 4 x 100-meter relay, even though she initially declined—she didn't consider herself to be very good at either sport. "Someone's got to do it so we can keep the item on our list! Plus, this is the first time we finally got two cohorts to compete against each other!"

As the lead organizer, Ouyang had a team of assistants, including Yanshao, to pull the entire event together. Jun was surprised to see the other side of Ouyang. Without his glasses, he was an entirely different person for sports—fearless, focused, and competitive.

Jun competed in the high jump on the first day. Among the four competitors, she got the silver medal. *Interesting! This is kind of fun,* she thought. It was her first medal ever from a sports competition.

When she wasn't competing, she was cheering for others, especially Yanshao. She noticed the same woman cheering for every sport she herself was supporting.

"Is there anyone in particular you're cheering for?" Jun asked during their third round of cheering.

The lady's face blushed. She pointed to Ouyang, "Him—but also everyone. How about you?"

Jun nodded at Yanshao and said, "Him, and everyone else. I'm Liu Jun, by the way."

"I'm Li Fanghua, one year ahead of you."

"Are you and Ouyang…?" Jun asked.

"We came from the same hometown, on the other side of the Blue Mountains. Our families are friends."

"Ah, similar. Yanshao and I came from the same hometown, far away from here."

Jun and Fanghua gave each other an understanding smile. They moved on to cheer at the next competition.

The last items on the second day were the ladies' 4 x 100 meters relay, followed by the men's. Each of these competitions were between the two cohorts. Jun's team asked her to be the last runner. "You're the tallest, with the longest legs. We trust you!" They said, despite Jun protesting, that she didn't run regularly and didn't know how fast she could run.

Beside her, standing on the next line, was Fanghua. *She's not tall, so the reason can't be that she has long legs. She must run faster than her teammates. But wait, Ouyang said this was the first time they're holding a relay race. So maybe she's like me and has never run a relay before.* Jun had learned from Yanshao that the fastest runners should be positioned either first or last in the relay.

The cheering grew louder as the runners began passing the baton to their teammates with each lap. Jun's heart raced and her body instinctively tensed in preparation. She fixed her gaze on the baton in her teammates' hands. When the third runner was about twenty meters from her, she moved her feet with a small run forward. She turned her head and saw in her peripheral vision as her teammate extended her left arm behind her, palm open to the sky. When the baton touched Jun's palm, she gripped it and sprinted forward with full force. There was only one thing in her mind: Run! Run as fast as you can!

The cheering from onlookers erupted into an enthusiastic roar as her chest brushed against a string of red yarn at the finish line. She slowed down and turned around just as Fanghua set foot on the finish line. She'd won! Her team had won!

There was no time to reflect or celebrate because Yanshao and Ouyang were heading into the last lap for the men's relay. She'd never cheered so hard. The crowd erupted when the two men reached the red yarn, only a hair's breadth apart, with Ouyang crossing the finish line first.

What a thrill those two days had been! Jun never thought of herself as athletic and had never been fond of any physical activities. Now she had a completely different view of sports. She thanked Yanshao for giving her all the tips about the relay.

***

On a Saturday afternoon, students gathered in the large lecture hall for the monthly political meeting, where the school administrators would provide guidance, make an announcement, or do something for "the health of the minds," as they claimed.

Yanshao, Jun, Ouyang, and Fanghua were sitting together. They had spent more time together as a group ever since the sports competition. As Jun chatted with Fanghua, she got a glimpse of Wu Dazhi sitting one row behind on her left, staring at her. She had seen him staring at her a few too many times—in classes, the canteen, or the playground. It made her uneasy.

"Students, I want to bring your attention to a serious matter." The school administration leader, Teacher Hao, cleared his throat.

People quieted down.

"This is a school for grownups. Your goal here is to study, get ready for the workforce, and prepare to contribute to our country's development. Everything you do should be to support this goal. Dating is prohibited because it can distract one's attention and negatively affect one's performance. Plus, our society doesn't appreciate public displays of affection because they're filthy and gross." He paused, his eyes quickly passing by each of the four of them. He shifted to a different topic then and continued speaking.

Jun's face burned. Her heart raced, her limbs grew heavy, and her mind became foggy. Teacher Hao's words sparked a deep shame. When was the last time she'd been accused of wrongdoing? Never. When was the last time she'd been so publicly humiliated? Never. She stared at her hands and heard nothing else for the rest of the meeting. That evening, she didn't go to the canteen for dinner. Later, she couldn't remember what she'd done on Sunday.

By Monday, her mind grew clearer. She didn't want people to associate her name with "those who dated in school." She would let people believe she and Yanshao came from the same hometown, but nothing more. She wanted others to see her in a positive light.

Jun joined the singing and dancing club, which was made up of about half women and half men. They trained for traditional Chinese dances and sang popular music influenced by revolutionary songs from the Soviet Union. They also performed on various special occasions, such as International Workers' Day in May, Army Establishing Day in July, National Day in October, and various traditional holidays like the Moon Festivals and New Year celebrations. She also discovered she enjoyed playing badminton. The sweat from two hours of play washed away her mental fatigue and lifted her spirits. She constantly looked for other ways to keep herself busy.

Yanshao didn't approach Jun in public, or privately. He understood Jun and regretted that their time together had caused Jun to feel uneasy.

Whenever he saw Jun in classes, the canteen, or on the field, he smiled and nodded at her the same way he would to anyone else. He kept himself busy with sports of all kinds. He also became an avid reader of many literary books from the library.

14

UNWANTED ATTENTION

The first winter break came, and the Spring Festival wasn't far off. Many students talked about going home for what was the biggest holiday of the year.

Yanshao casually approached Jun in the canteen one day when she was about to leave her table. Sitting down quietly, he said, "I'm going to go home to see my mom. What's your plan for the break? I don't think it'll be a problem if we go home together. Ouyang and Fanghua are leaving together, even though their home is so close by."

Jun wasn't fond of hearing the mention of Ouyang and Fanghua together as a unit. It was the association she wanted nothing to do with. But when she looked at Yanshao, her heart filled with warmth. It had been a while since she'd really focused on him.

She said softly, "Xia is visiting Xi-Dan and his wife. So I'll stay here for the holiday."

Jun had missed Xia so much and hoped to be back to see her. She wouldn't want Xia to spend the holiday alone. It had been hard enough for Xia to be by herself for the past several months. But when Jun counted her leftover savings, she realized she wouldn't have enough for train tickets and food during the visit. By then, Xia had written her a letter saying Xi-Dan had invited her and Jun to spend the holiday with him in his new place, which was a few hours from Chifeng by bus.

"You're staying? Here? For the holiday?" Yanshao was concerned, his eyebrows raised.

"Yeah, where else would I go?" Jun murmured. Xi-Dan had invited her, too, but she didn't want to mention the money shortage to Yanshao.

Yanshao continued to stare at her. "You could, you know, come to..." He wished he could bring her to his home for the holiday.

"From what I understand, a few others will stay, too. I'll have company." Jun gave a slight smile. "Have a good time with your mom. She must be missing you so much. Pass my regards to her and wish her a Happy New Year."

Seven students stayed at the school, two girls and five boys. They gathered for meals. Wu Dazhi was one of them. The first two days, he sat away from Jun, quiet and focused on his meals. Jun figured he was an introvert, even nerdy, recalling him from some of their classes. He hardly ever raised his hand. But in the labs, he'd helped some fellow students with their tasks. His name popped up here and there when the teachers announced the best performers in exams or housework.

On the third day, Dazhi began sitting one seat away or across the table from Jun. He was still quiet, and his gaze was still intense. A few times, he joined conversations at the table and said a few witty and funny things, making several of the students pause, look at each other, and laugh in amusement. Whenever that would happen,

Dazhi would glance at Jun with a searching eye to see if Jun had appreciated whatever he'd said.

Jun had appreciated his humor and cleverness. But she was also uneasy. She sensed from the very beginning of school that Dazhi paid more attention to her than to any other ladies. This wasn't the type of attention she wanted at all. Too bad they had to spend the holiday on campus together.

Jun became cautious. She avoided looking at Dazhi and avoided reacting to anything he said or did. She lowered her head whenever he was around.

On the eve of the Spring Festival, Teacher Hao invited the seven students to his house for dumplings, a traditional food for celebrating the Chinese New Year. Hao's wife had already prepared the dough and stuffing. Students helped make dumplings. Jun volunteered to make dumpling skins. At home, she was a quick and skilled dumpling skin maker who could keep three people busy with wrapping. Dazhi stood quietly by her, picking up the round skins and quickly wrapping the stuffing into a neat shape—it was clear he had done it before. The proximity made Jun self-conscious. The occasional touch of their elbows made her tremble.

"Hey, Jun. How could you make a triangular skin?" one student asked jokingly, holding a skin with folded edges.

"Are you okay?" Teacher Hao's wife asked, noticing Jun's sweat on her forehead.

"I'm going to take a break. Could you take over, please?" Jun said to the lady.

Jun went to the washbowl stand to wash her hands. When she was reaching for a towel on the washbowl stand, the towel was in front of her already—Dazhi was holding it.

"Are you sick?" He asked gently.

Jun almost jumped. She looked at Dazhi, freaked out and speechless. She didn't hear him coming so close.

Dazhi gestured with the towel. Jun turned around and wiped her hands on her pants. She wanted to shout. But to what end? Would anyone understand her? What kind of reaction would she get from people, especially Teacher Hao?

She walked toward a desk and sat down in the chair, mindlessly looking at the books in front of her.

Jun didn't know how long it was until Teacher Hao's wife came over to tell her dinner was ready. The round table was too small, and the rest of the nine people squeezed in, elbow to elbow. Several big plates of dumplings were in the middle, thick steam going to the ceiling. Two bottles of rice vinegar were in the middle too. Each person had a small bowl and a pair of chopsticks, eager to taste the fruits of their labor.

Jun sat by Teacher Hao's wife. She'd lost her appetite. She could sense Dazhi's stare from across the table. Teacher Hao's wife put a few dumplings in her bowl and said, "Eat while they're still hot. You must be hungry."

Walking back to their dormitory, Jun tried hard to stay far away from Dazhi. For the next three days, the canteen reduced to two meals per day to give the cooks a break. It was a welcome change for Jun. She didn't have to see Dazhi as frequently. For the rest of the break, Jun reduced the number of times she had to venture out for meals by stashing food in her room. It was cold outside, making any activities hard. Jun only went out twice to ice skate. The rest of the time, she kept herself busy in her room. This was the perfect time for her to make clothes and shoes for herself and Xia for the year to come.

Dazhi must have gotten the message, as he no longer tried to approach Jun.

Jun was still relieved when all the students had come back, and the new semester started.

A few weeks into the semester, a teacher grouped students into pairs for a physics lab. To Jun's horror, she was partnered with Dazhi. To complete the task, each pair of students had to work together for two hours, every other day for two weeks.

Jun felt deeply conflicted. She wanted to do well on the assignment, which required her to work well with her lab partner. But she also wanted to avoid Dazhi. She came to the lab early to do her part and hoped to leave early. But that would not do, insisted the teacher. Both partners had to do the work together.

The first week went by unremarkably as Jun tiptoed around, keeping her head down, and speaking only when it was absolutely necessary.

The following Monday, when she came to the lab at their designated time, she found Dazhi there already, sitting in a chair, sobbing.

That shocked Jun. Her first thought was that something bad had happened to Dazhi or to his family. She hurried over to him, asking, "Are you alright?"

He raised his head as tears rolled down his cheeks. Jun thought she had never seen a boy crying like this. Not her brothers, not Yanshao, not anyone she knew. She looked at him patiently, waiting to hear what he would say. At the moment, he looked like such an innocent little boy.

"I'm sorry I scared you." He wiped his face with one sleeve. "I didn't mean to hurt you at all. It's just... It's just, that whenever I see your beautiful face, I can't help myself, I keep looking at you. I really like you, and it pains me to see how scared you are of me."

Jun had not expected this confession. She just stood there and did not know what to do.

Dazhi stood up from the chair, and Jun automatically backed a step from him. His sobbing started again.

"Shh. Hey, you stop." Jun tried to find the right words. The silence felt so awkward. Her fear faded as she began to pity the boy.

Dazhi stopped, looking at her with hope in his eyes.

Jun struggled to find the right words that would stop that hope in its tracks. "I'm not... I don't... I don't like when people stare at me."

Dazhi's eyes moved from her face to his feet.

"Can we... can we just focus on studying like Teacher Hao told us? Let's do our lab work." Jun moved to the table where they were about to start their assignment.

Dazhi wiped his face with his other sleeve and didn't say a single word after that. It was a productive session.

The next day, Jun didn't see Dazhi in classes. On Wednesday, he didn't show up at their usual project time. Jun finished the task on her own, but felt worried. Dazhi seemed like a serious student and not showing up for classes or teamwork wasn't like him. Jun went to Teacher Hao's office.

"Is everything alright with Wu Dazhi? He missed classes and our team meeting today," she inquired.

"Is that so? I haven't heard anything. I'll look into it," replied Teacher Hao.

There was still no sign of Dazhi for the rest of the week. The following Monday, buzzes were around the canteen. Jun sat down at her regular table with several regular female friends.

"I heard Wu Dazhi left." One of them said.

"Left? Where did he go?" Jun became alarmed.

"Home. He's only the second student ever to leave the school. The other one was from the first cohort; health reasons," the young woman responded.

Jun knocked on Teacher Hao's office in the afternoon.

"Just the person I want to speak with," he said when he saw her.

"Does this have to do with Dazhi?" Jun asked carefully.

"Yes. Dazhi wasn't in a good place when I talked to him last week. He told me he hadn't eaten and couldn't do anything for days. He said he felt bad about scaring you. By the way, both my wife and I thought you looked uneasy at my home on New Year's Eve. It makes sense now."

Jun gazed at him. She didn't know where this was going.

Teacher Hao continued, "He developed feelings for you and that affected him badly. Given his condition, I suggested he take a break from school. Once he recovers, we can have him back in a new academic year."

Jun was speechless. She never imagined that Dazhi's situation could be this bad, and it made her feel awful.

Teacher Hao spoke slowly, "He said it hurt him the most when you told him you disliked his attention. But none of this is your fault. You did the right thing."

Jun left Teacher Hao's office, her mind in turmoil. A bright young student's future had been halted—perhaps even ruined. Could she have done something different to prevent this? She searched her memory, recalling their first meeting at the train station and the cart ride to campus. If she had been cold and hadn't spoken to him that day, would any of this have happened? If she hadn't told Teacher Hao about Dazhi missing classes, would he still be in school?

Watch your actions, your words, and how you interact with others! She silently ordered herself.

Wu Dazhi never returned before Jun graduated.

15

VISITS

During the summer of 1957, Xia came to visit before starting high school. She wished she could visit Jun more often during holidays and school breaks. Time and travel discomforts were less of a concern than the money needed for the tickets. Besides relying on some of Jun's allowance, Xia landed two jobs at her high school—a teacher's assistant and a canteen helper—but the income from those jobs barely covered her meals. Similar to middle school, she lived in a free schoolroom and shared it with another homeless girl.

"You've grown at least another three centimeters!" Jun exclaimed, noticing the new womanly curves of Xia's body. Most women had flat chests. Xia's breasts stood out like two small hills. She had wide shoulders, but her waist was small, and her hips narrow. Her rosy face was round with tender jaw lines, and her lips were full and thick. When she grinned, her bright red lips surrounded neat white teeth. Xia had grown into an attractive young woman.

"It helps with shooting baskets," Xia grinned.

"You look like a basketball player, one of those tall and muscular ones. Still playing a lot?"

"Yes, every day. Where's Yanshao?"

Jun led Xia to the canteen. "We'll see him there. I told him you were coming."

Yanshao stood by a table, expectantly looking at the entry. His eyes widened and a broad grin spread across his face when he saw Xia. There was an "I can't believe it" expression on his face and it was obvious he admired what he saw. Xia was smiling, too, and bounded to Yanshao's side with a few quick, long steps.

"Hey, look at you!" Yanshao greeted Xia. "All grown up—and so tall."

"Let's see who's taller!" Xia stood back-to-back with Yanshao.

Jun reported, "You're about the same height."

People looked their way, staring at Xia in admiration. "Your sister, Jun?" someone asked. "Yes," Jun answered proudly.

"I guess you're still playing basketball," Yanshao said, gazing at Xia.

"Yes, daily. How about you? Anything else you've been doing?" Xia took a big bite of a steamed bun. She had been hungry. *Her manner is still childish,* Jun thought.

"Yes, daily. And I do other sports—field activities and running. Anything I can get my hands and feet on."

"Same here!" Xia extended her hand, and Yanshao shook it.

"How about we play some ball after the meal?" Yanshao suggested. Then he looked at Jun with an apologetic expression and added, "Only if it doesn't interfere with what your sister has planned for you."

Jun watched what was happening, a mix of emotions swirling inside her. Part of her felt happy and proud, while another part was uneasy. Her sister was getting a lot of attention from everyone, which was understandable and made her proud. But Xia also had Yanshao's full attention—or perhaps they were both equally absorbed in each other. Although they'd been as close as family members before and they hadn't seen each other for a long year, Jun sensed there was something more.

Maybe you're being over-sensitive. He saved her life when she had appendicitis. They're as close as a brother and sister would be.

Jun silently shook her head to push away unpleasant feelings. She put more food in Xia's bowl and said, "No plans. You guys shoot baskets all you like."

The next day, Jun showed Xia the campus. They also visited the old town of Hohhot. Everything impressed Xia. They got back in time to catch the tail end of dinner.

"Where's Yanshao? Why doesn't he join us for dinner?" Xia looked around.

"He must have plans." Jun gestured for Xia to eat before the food got cold.

"Are you guys still together? I sensed yesterday you hadn't talked to each other awhile."

Jun was amused. Her insensitive sister was in fact quite sensitive.

"The school doesn't allow boys and girls to spend time together unless it's for work or study."

"Nonsense. You two are like family," Xia protested.

"Shh. Are you done with eating? We still need to get some hot water after this."

At the end of the visit, Xia was sad. "I've missed you and Yanshao so much. Maybe I'll come again during the next Spring Festival."

Jun passed Xia an envelope. "Here's extra money for you to buy bras and sneakers."

"Oh good. I need bras. My chest hurts when I run and jump."

"Maybe you should save the train ticket money and don't visit too often. The money could buy you two pairs of sneakers."

Xia almost cried. Jun continued, "Plus, you need to focus on studying so you can make it to college. We've worked so hard to get here and you should not waste all our efforts."

"I know. I'll do my best."

Xia's next visit would be a big surprise for Jun.

***

On a bright Sunday morning of fall 1958, Jun was walking back to her dorm with two hot water bottles. Fall came after the brief summer season and lasted about three months before the ice of winter arrived. Jun couldn't believe this was the third and last year of her study. Having finished a week of heavy schoolwork, she had little else scheduled for today.

From a distance, she saw two figures standing by her dorm door. She recognized immediately one of them was Xia, taller than she'd been on her last visit. She had a schoolbag that crossed her upper body. The other was a grown man in his early 30s. A duffel bag stood by his feet.

He was slightly taller than Xia, with a military haircut showing his square forehead, and his square shoulders pulled back in disciplined habit. His square jaw lines reminded her of her father's—they seemed to smile at her as she drew nearer. Those eyes! They were just like Jun's or her dad's. They were so familiar.

Jun's heart pounded. She rushed over and tossed down the water bottles. She stood in front of him and examined his face with such intensity.

"Hello, Junjun," said the man in a deep mellow voice that reminded her again of her father. He stared back at her with the same intensity but a smiling face.

"You? You! Where have you been all these years?" Jun wasn't sure what had come out of her mouth or even what should come. So many memories and emotions overwhelmed her. Her brother! Her favorite big brother was standing in front of her!

"It's a long story to tell. Shall we find a place to sit and eat? Xia and I just came from the train station." Xi-Chang bent down and picked up the water bottles.

"And you! You didn't warn me," Jun turned to Xia.

"Umm, I didn't have time. Big brother showed up yesterday and we caught the first train from Chifeng to here," Xia murmured.

Jun opened the door, took the bottles from Xi-Chang, put them down, then came back out.

"The canteen is closed for breakfast. Let's go to that diner outside the school." She led them to the diner she had visited once to celebrate an upper classmate's job placement.

Xi-Chang ordered tea and food.

Jun sat down, putting her hands on her cheeks, unable to take her eyes off her brother.

"Now tell me, first, where are you now? Where do you live?"

"I live in Shijiazhuang, in Hebei province."

"It's near Beijing," said Jun.

"Relatively speaking, yes, not far." Xi-Chang sipped some tea and picked up a steamed bun.

"For how long?" Jun followed.

"About a year now since I retired from the military. Before that, I was in a place I shouldn't mention because of security reasons."

"Is that why you never contacted us? Because you were in the military?"

"Yes, and no. Well, it's a long story and I'm not able to tell you much about it. But I'm here now." Xi-Chang spoke slowly, which also reminded Jun of her father, who never rushed when he spoke. She hadn't expected her brother to be so much like her father. He even called her "Junjun," the name only her father used. Jun appreciated Xi-Chang's gesture of bringing the old days back.

"You were 16 when you left home," Jun gushed.

"Yes, young and dumb." Xi-Chang smiled awkwardly.

"And you would be... how old now? 28?" Jun calculated. He was five years older than her. But he looked much older than 28. Life must have been tough on him, Jun thought.

"Yes, 28, older but not much wiser," Xi-Chang said humbly.

"Now, tell me a little what happened after you left home. I've imagined so many possibilities for so many years," Jun said. She had missed him so much without really even realizing it. So many times, she'd wondered what would have happened if Xi-Chang had never married Meiling. Would her family have ended up in a different situation? But she knew she would never know. And she knew she would never mention Meiling's name—she was certain it would hurt him too much to be reminded of what had happened after the fatal morning when he'd beaten Meiling in front of the family.

"Sure, I can tell you. We were stationed in a place I didn't know. We trained daily and did what we were told to do. Not much actual fighting, more like being stationed at places as guards. One day, our commander said we would surrender to the People's Liberation Army. Soon after, the new China was established."

"For years, I was worried you could be in Taiwan." Jun exhaled. It was one of her fears. An association with anyone in Taiwan was one of the worst possible associations.

"It was a possibility. Many of Chiang Kai-Shek's army escaped to Taiwan with him. But the branch I was in didn't. We were considered heroes for protecting Beijing from being destroyed by a potential battle." Xi-Chang's body relaxed, and he sipped some more tea.

"Great. So, you weren't negatively affected by joining Chiang Kai-Shek's National Army."

"Not at all. Along with many of my comrades, I got promoted. Well, that's another story I can't get too detailed about."

"What kind of job do you do now?" Jun was fine with not knowing some parts of Xi-Chang's journey.

"I'm a technician of machinery. I produce parts that are used by many large tools or machines."

"Why didn't you visit us sooner?" Jun couldn't help it. She knew it hadn't just been her—Xia and Xi-Dan had missed Xi-Chang, too.

"Well, it took me a while to find you guys," responded Xi-Chang.

True, Jun thought. Xia was the only one in Chifeng now and she didn't live in the family house.

"It took two trips to Chifeng to find Xia. Many old neighbors and friends weren't to be found anywhere. Anyhow, now I've reconnected with you. Xi-Dan is next." Xi-Chang's warm smile was so much like a big brother's smile.

"It's too bad Xi-Dan isn't here with us," Xia interjected, her hunger satiated.

Jun said, "Xi-Dan came to visit during his spring break a few months ago. It was only for one day. But I'm grateful he took the time and effort to come. Oh—he remarried and is busy teaching at a middle school. He's also in Hebei province. You two aren't far from each other."

"Yes, I heard from Xia. I plan to visit him after I leave here. I wanted to visit you first." Xi-Chang's words warmed Jun. When they were young and at home, Jun was a pet of Xi-Chang's and Xia was Xi-Dan's. That hadn't changed, it seemed.

"Good, you can visit him. He looked happy and healthy. He also showed me his wife's picture. She's also a teacher. She looked fine, nothing striking." Jun swallowed and realized she shouldn't impose her opinions of her sister-in-law on him. After all, Xi-Dan seemed to love this lady and spoke highly of her, unlike his first wife Peifang. Jun silently scorned at the thought of Peifang.

Back in the here and now, Jun continued, "By the way, you two look nothing alike now. Well, you never did even when you were young." Jun smiled and recalled those fond days when they were all so young and happy. It was such a long time ago.

"I want to know what he looks like now. Did you take a picture when he visited?" Xi-Chang asked.

"Oh, yes, we did," Jun nodded. "I'll find it when we get back."

"And if you're finished eating," Xi-Chang nodded at Xia and the empty plates, "we should go to the photo shop."

It had become a tradition to take a photo of each family visit. They didn't get to see each other frequently, and the photos kept their memories alive.

16

JOB PREPARATION

The Anti-Rightest Campaign, which began in 1957, was based on the idea that one's political position was more important than one's academic performance. Openly disagreeing with the communist party was a big no-no. Openly showing support in words or deeds garnered praise. The school administration constantly reminded students to maintain "correct" political positions. "Know which side you're on! You should aim to be correct politically and competent professionally." They said so in meetings and hung banners with these slogans around campus.

Jun showed a strong alignment with the party. She organized several events, following the party's calls to action. By her second year in school, she was voted by her peers and selected by the school's administration to be the officer of the Communist Youth League, an organization for youngsters that mirrored the communist party for grownups. Her name was everywhere.

One day in the canteen, Jun overheard someone saying, "Doesn't the name seem old-fashioned?" She wasn't sure who they were talking about, but she felt self-conscious about her name.

The current character, meaning a gentleman, is old-fashioned. No one cares if someone has good manners or not. But people care whether a person is on the Red side (a member of the Communist Youth League or Communist Party) or the Black side (e.g. anti-party, rightists, and the lowest classes). What about another character—it has the same sound, but it means army? This character would imply I'm a soldier who'll fight for the party. It'll be obvious which side I'm on.

Liu Jun 刘君 → Liu Jun 刘军

She requested the name change and received overwhelming support, not only from the school leaders but also from her peers. Several students followed suit and changed their names, too.

The next political movement was the Great Leap Forward Campaign, which started in 1958. The entire country was motivated to answer the party's calls for the economic collectivization of agriculture and the realization of socialism. In school, students had field trips to local farms and factories, reinforcing their sense of duty to follow the Communist Party's directives and contribute to the nation's most critical sectors after graduation.

The school's first cohort was about to graduate! Spring 1958 was all about jobs—the topic dominated conversations among students and even among teachers. It was rumored students from the engineering school were in great demand, and all students would get employment upon graduation. People were also told all jobs were placed based on the needs of the country, and the school would work with the local and higher-level governments to match job positions with graduates.

Students could fill in a job request form. There were sections on the form where they could specify if there was a geographical location they preferred to go, or if there was someone they preferred to be placed together with.

"But what does this mean? Will the school consider these requests?" One student raised his hand during the all-school meeting on jobs.

"This is a generic form by the provincial government. Some students are eager to go to the most underserved and impoverished areas. This form allows them to voice their desires," said Teacher Hao.

"How does the match process work? What are the criteria to match someone to a particular position?" another student asked.

"We'll follow the guidelines from the government when the time comes," said Teacher Hao.

"Do we know what positions are available?" a third person asked.

"Yes. I'm going to read out the ones we have right now, but there will be more to come." Teacher Hao cleared his throat and started reading out a few details—the name of the organization and its geographical location—of about twenty open positions. Students were less familiar with the organizations but more familiar with the locations.

Excitement expanded the campus. People knew how important a job was. It would provide an opportunity to apply what they learned to contribute to the country—as they were told again and again. It would secure a steady livelihood with a salary based on education level. Holding a prestigious job would bring pride and respect from others. A job's location could also imply the type of lifestyle it might offer. Secretly, people preferred big cities and wished to avoid marginal places with less civilization.

More jobs came in and were posted on the bulletin board in the canteen. The list stopped at 29, the exact number of graduates.

Anxiety filled the student body. Some students loudly voiced their observations and opinions, some were quiet.

"Geez, 29 holes to be filled by 29 students, not a single extra."

"Some people will be luckier than others, that's for sure."

"This is going to mean some competition among the 29 students."

The job placement announcement day was a big day at the school. All three cohorts filled the lecture hall.

The audience clapped each time Teacher Hao read off a student's name and their job placement.

When Ouyang and Fanghua's names were announced together, many students made an "Ooh" sound and smiled at the couple who sat next to each other. This made them the first publicly announced couple. The audience went silent after Teacher Hao had read out their job placements. Some students murmured to their neighbors. Some looked disgusted. Several shook their heads. The two placements were close to each other in a marginal and severely underdeveloped area.

A few names later, another couple's names and jobs became public. Unlike Ouyang and Fanghua, most people, including Jun, hadn't known they were a couple. Like Ouyang and Fanghua, this couple got placed in similar marginal regions—far away from any big cities.

It was clear at this point that Teacher Hao was no longer enjoying reading the list, but he had to keep going.

Someone made a loud cough sound as if to request an explanation.

Teacher Hao wiped his sweating forehead after reading off the last placement.

"As you have seen already, our school has many demands from all geographical locations and various types of institutes. Someone has to go to those less desirable places. If you want to be together, we'll satisfy your requests, but you'll likely end up in those less desirable places. But you all should follow what our country asks of you, whether your request is met."

The two couples had become the unlucky bearers of bad news.

"Did anyone get to go where they wished to go?" a lady next to Jun whispered.

"I heard one did, although his family is in a rural town and few people without connections there would find it attractive," Jun answered.

The job placements of that first cohort cast a shadow on the later cohorts.

Jun's heart was heavy, too. It was hard to figure out the criteria besides the ones yielding the obvious outcome for the two couples. Jun did notice, however, that some of the better students seemed to get posted to institutes whose names were impressive and specific.

Jun kept her observations to herself.

Landing a desirable job became the primary goal for Jun. With that as her north star, she conducted herself carefully. Never a loud-mouth before, she became even more reticent now, never expressing her opinions freely. She tried her best to be a pleasant person, but maintained a safe distance, never too close, and not too far out of reach. She didn't want to draw any more unnecessary attention that might have ill consequences. Jun studied hard and became the top student in all her classes. She stayed politically active by saying and doing the right things. She stood out from the crowd, and in a positive way.

17

JOB PLACEMENT

1959 came. It was time to submit requests for job placements. Contrary to the way they'd done it the year before, the school didn't publicize the positions. There was no information on how many positions, nor what or where they were. The school said they had more positions this year because of last year's successful job placements.

In the canteen, Yanshao quietly sat down by Jun. "Can I assume you won't submit a request?"

Jun looked at him, his face clouded over.

"We'd better not. Remember Ouyang and Fanghua?"

"Of course, and the other couple, too." Yanshao lowered his head for a moment, then looked at Jun again. "We'll have to see what fate may bring us."

"Yes, we'll have to wait and see. It seems no request is best. Any attention now would be unwelcome attention," Jun murmured.

Yanshao thought for a moment but said nothing. He stood up and left the table.

Jun sat there, watching his back disappearing by the door. He was still the most handsome man in the entire school. Although he wasn't as politically active as Jun was, he remained one of the few all-A students and one of the top all-sports athletes.

Jun sent a prayer.

Lao-Tian-Ye. Please put us in the same institute if you can. Or put us in the same city. Or not too far from each other. I beg you!

Their cohorts' job placements were posted on the bulletin board in the canteen. On the top of the list was Jun. She was to join a top civil engineering institute located right here in Hohhot. It was widely known as the best among all the institutes listed. When they discovered it was in fact the best institute in the entire country for the jobs they'd be doing, many jaws dropped. Few believed the placement was unjustified, and many hoped they might have a chance there in the future.

Yanshao's job was in a small rural town.

"It's unfair. You should have gotten a better position or location," Jun said furiously as they walked out of the canteen.

"Teacher Hao asked me not to share this with others. But I can tell you—just keep it to yourself." He looked around, making sure no one was nearby to hear him.

"Teacher Hao knew about us. He said if I wanted, I could choose between two jobs because the school got over 30 positions. The school first assigned me to an institute in Harbin. He said the institute was one of the best and my performance deserved it. But he wanted to see if I'd prefer a location closer to you. No other jobs were inside Hohhot. This one was the closest, a few hours by bus. It's in a critical place where the dam is important to the nearby community, and it constantly needs monitoring and maintenance. The town has requested a graduate two years in a row now."

Harbin was a city in the northeast region bordering Russia. It was a lot colder than Chifeng and very far from Hohhot.

Jun looked at Yanshao in silence. The warmth from her heart unfurled throughout her body. All these years in school, they could only give each other a knowing look, an understanding nod, and a few absolutely necessary words in public. But their bond was still strong. And now, Yanshao had made a sacrifice. Jun's mouth moved, but she couldn't find any proper words to say. Her eyes grew moist with tears.

Yanshao studied her emotional expression and grinned. "Congratulations! I'm so proud of you."

18

RISING STAR

On the first day she arrived at the institute, Jun met Mimi, who had graduated from a top-tier technology university in the northeastern region. They were the same height, had similarly shaped slim bodies, and looked the same age. Mimi was a pretty girl as well. When their division director introduced them to each other, explaining that they would be on the same team and share the same dormitory room, Mimi shot Jun a look that oozed superiority and the desire to stand apart. Jun wondered if it was the mention of vocational school that had lowered her in Mimi's estimation. Whatever the reason, Jun had seen the expression many times in the past, plastered on the faces of girls from richer families with fancier clothes, and on boys who didn't believe she could do better than them in school.

Jun faced Mimi with a friendly smile. Mimi paused and gave Jun a slight nod.

She's an ice queen, Jun thought.

When they moved into their room, Jun let Mimi pick the more desirable bed away from the door. Mimi nodded again and the ice on her face melted a little. Jun couldn't help but notice that Mimi had very little luggage.

"How do you live with almost nothing? Few clothes, no extra bedding?" Jun was curious.

"My stuff is at home. My parents live in the old town section of Hohhot."

"How lucky you are to be so close to your family." Jun sensed a sour taste in her mouth.

"Yes, at last. I missed them badly while I was away at college."

"Why did you go far away to college? There are good ones here locally, like Inner Mongolia University."

"My dad said attending college locally may not guarantee a good local job. People value those who hail from other places. You know, the notion, 'An outside monk is a better monk.' My goal was to live close to my parents when I found a job. I'm grateful I'm here. But my husband couldn't find a job locally."

"Where is he?"

"He's in Changchun."

"Oh, no!" Changchun was far from Hohhot, even farther than Chifeng. In comparison, she was glad Yanshao was only a few hours away by bus.

"I know. We didn't make any requests for job placement. At least I got to my hometown, and he's in a big city, not a rural area."

"We didn't either," Jun murmured.

"You're married too?"

"No. Well, not at all. He's my classmate. We came from the same hometown and have known each other for six years. He got a job a few hours from here."

"It might be a smart thing to do. I mean, not get married. I didn't listen to my dad and got the marriage license secretly, thinking it was so romantic."

"Do you regret getting married?"

"No, that's not what I mean. Not living together freaked me out."

"Did you tell the institute you're married?"

"Yes, I can't lie on the profile where they ask if I'm married. They know my husband is remote. It might be the reason I'm sharing the room with you, instead of having a unit for married people."

The institute provided housing for all employees. The singles dormitory was a two-story building, where women occupied several rooms upstairs. Roughly twenty percent of the employees were women and about half of them lived in the singles dormitory, either because they were unmarried or because they lived separately from their spouses.

Jun and Mimi had been on the same projects from the beginning. In the first in-house project, Jun sensed a hierarchical structure to the team, and she was at the bottom. She was the only one without a college degree. Maybe it was the reason her job was to assist others, including Mimi, who got assigned specific tasks. Anyone on the team could call her and delegate some minor task to Jun. She didn't like it. She wanted to be treated equally, like Mimi and the other college graduates. At institute meetings, Jun learned she wasn't the only one. The institute had a tradition of forming hierarchical teams for each project. The leaders openly said, "Prove yourself. Prove where you belong. You start somewhere, but you may not end at the same place in the hierarchy. We evaluate your performance frequently."

In the first remote project, a team of two women, Jun and Mimi, and six men went to a place three days' travel away—a train, multiple long-distance buses, and horse- and donkey-drawn carts. There was no civilization—no buildings of any kind, no utility poles, not even any trees. There were only rocky hills and a valley where a river ran through.

They set up two tents in a relatively flat place by a hill to block the wind. Jun and Mimi used one tent to set up their camp beds, each a foldable metal frame with a pad for a single person to lie down in one position only. If a person wanted to change positions on the bed, she'd fall to the ground.

There were no cooked meals. They had to eat dry food or canned food. To get fresh water, one of them had to take a bucket and walk down the hill for over 20 minutes to fetch water from the stream. They boiled the water on a portable stove to make it drinkable, then filled the water bottles they'd be carrying the next day. When it got dark, they used covered oil lamps for lighting, which were a lot more affordable than candles. Plus, people could carry them around without the risk of setting clothing or tents on fire. The guys' tent was larger and held all six of them. At night, Jun and Mimi could hear their loud snores, as if there was a concert next door.

Once settled, the team immediately started working. The sooner they could finish, the sooner they could return home. Everyone was eager to work hard. Their task was to gather raw data about the surroundings, do measurements and calculations, and draft a feasibility report for a dam to be built along the river.

Jun was called upon to record measurements. Though not winter yet, her hands became cold and tired quickly. She had trouble holding a pencil still or writing legibly. Sometimes she worried she might slow down progress because the readings came faster than she could write them down. Jun was also called upon to hold devices at targeted spots so others could detect the devices from a distance, which was one method of measuring. Such spots were at the worst possible locations: no shade for sun, no shelter for rain, and not enough flat ground to stand properly. She'd have to get on all fours, carrying a device and balancing her body to get to a proper spot. The team leader kindly spared her from climbing to high places after he learned she was afraid of heights. Once they all returned to the tents and had supper, they'd compare notes, do paperwork, and plan out the next day's tasks.

On the third day, Mimi couldn't get up in the morning. Her menstrual cramps were so bad she rolled on the ground and moaned with tears. "Does this happen a lot?" Jun asked. "Not really," Mimi moaned. "Maybe only once a year. It must be the cold water I drank yesterday."

When the team leader made the second call for work, Jun told him Mimi couldn't work. "Did she bring any medicine for such a condition?" he asked. Jun knew Mimi hadn't, or she'd have taken it already.

The team leader said to both of them, "Newbies. This is your first time doing remote work. Always prepare for the worst. Now, Jun, you take over Mimi's task. Ask Mimi to brief you."

On the third and final call for work, Jun was ready for the task after Mimi filled her in. She left Mimi in the tent and went out with the guys. They spent the entire day out, bringing food and water bottles. Once back in the tents, the team leader summarized the day's work and praised Jun for doing a great job.

The next day, Mimi still couldn't work. Jun took over and again won praise.

By the time Mimi returned to work, Jun was doing tasks the team leader assigned to her.

At the end of the three weeks, the team was ready to go home.

"I can't thank you enough," Mimi said sincerely.

"Don't mention it. We all have difficult days and struggles."

Jun was happy about the outcome of the first remote project. Not only did she now understand firsthand the work she'd heard so much about at the vocational school, but she had also learned about teamwork and felt close to her co-workers. She'd gained confidence in doing independent tasks just like the college graduates did.

19

HELLO

It was the late fall of 1961. Jun set her luggage down in her dormitory and headed for the bathhouse inside the compound of the institute. In the last six months, she had only washed herself with a towel in her tent. A team of ten male and three female engineers had completed another project in the middle of nowhere. The team's charge was to verify a feasibility report and design a bridge over a wide river.

This had been her third remote project since she started working almost two years ago. The institute sent men or childless women engineers to remote projects. The projects could last between several weeks, such as for a quick feasibility study, to a couple of years, such as supervising the construction of a dam, building, or bridge.

In between remote projects, Jun got assigned to work on in-house projects. She earned praise constantly for being able to learn quickly, being diligent and detail-oriented, and delivering high-quality work.

Word spread, and team leaders frequently requested Jun for their teams, whether remote or in-house. Gradually, some leaders became comfortable letting Jun carry significant responsibilities for a project that would normally have been the responsibility of a seasoned engineer.

On the political side, Jun was doing well, too. Barely one year after she joined, she was voted to be the lead officer of the institute's Communist Youth League. In the following year, there was a noticeable increase in activities among young people. Many of them were away from their families. Such activities made them less lonely and more engaged.

All this made Jun proud. Her confidence had grown, and she felt a strong sense of control over her life.

The bath rejuvenated Jun. It was as if she'd taken off a heavy coat at the end of a long winter. She was light on her feet and smiling from the inside out. Her shoulder-length hair was wet and down instead of in pigtails, as most women had. Her creamy skin shone, and her face was rosy. Those big, dark eyes sparkled with excitement. She was ready for the evening's dance party. She had earned a three-day vacation for doing remote work, and she had made plans to visit Yanshao. Their last visit had been almost seven months ago. Their monthly letters were the only things they could hold on to of each other. Each time she mailed a letter, her heart and mind would long for a letter from Yanshao. The thought of visiting him warmed Jun's heart and made her smile.

"Oh, sorry!" Jun almost bumped into a tall figure in the bathhouse lobby.

"Excuse me. I should be more careful." A deep and mellow voice boomed out of the wide chest at Jun's eye level.

Jun stepped back and looked up. She stared at him for a long time without realizing what she was doing.

He was so tall! His face was angular, with sharp edges everywhere, as if a knife had carved it. The square cheek lines led to a pointy chin with a deep dimple at the end. His mouth was slightly open, and his lips were thin and tense. His nose bridge was high and straight. The dark brown eyes were long and narrow, with single eyelids. His long eyebrows stood out as if a bold brush of calligraphy had painted them in black ink. His forehead was a wide and tall rectangle, and his straight black hair was short and parted on one side, showing a neat hairline.

Bin-Kai was examining Jun with amazement, too. He saw a vibrant beauty standing in a beam of autumn sunshine that poured from the window. She looked like she was from another world, different from all the ladies he had met in the last five months since he joined the institute. She looked about 18, though her eyes showed she was much more mature. Those eyes. *Oh, my goodness.* He couldn't look away from her eyes. He saw so much there—they were clear and deep and revealed a rich inner world.

A fake cough brought both of them back into reality. A middle-aged man shrugged his shoulders to pass Bin-Kai and went to the door labeled "Men."

"Pardon me. My name is Zhou Bin-Kai. Glad to meet you." He stepped inside from the lobby door. With a slight hesitation, he extended his right hand.

"Nice to meet you. My name is Liu Jun." She shook his hand quickly. But she couldn't withdraw her hand because he held onto it. She blushed. Men and women weren't supposed to hold hands in public. Handshaking should be very brief, if at all.

"Do you work here or are you someone's daughter? I haven't seen you before." He looked deep into her eyes.

"I work here. Almost two years now. Just came back from a remote project." Her voice was steady now. She used a bit more force to take her hand out of his. He let her. She didn't know what to say next, so she turned around and was about to walk through the door when he spoke again.

"I'll see you around. I work here too. Oh, are you coming to the dance party tonight?"

She looked back over her shoulder at him. "See you there."

What was that about? Jun shook her head and frowned. *But he was so good-looking. No, so handsome.* She examined her right hand and recalled his grip. Her heart fluttered.

Jun went back to her room. Mimi was about to step out to visit her family.

"The room is all yours!" Mimi winked at her. In the past, she'd volunteered to visit her family when Jun had visitors, which was rare.

"Thanks. No one's going to visit me—I'm going to be doing the visiting."

Jun spent the afternoon on domestic chores—doing laundry, cleaning the room and bed, sewing buttons, and mending tears on her clothes. None of these could distract her from a vivid tableau in her mind's eye—the bathhouse lobby scene playing on repeat.

The big canteen could easily seat 200 people. All single people and many married people and their families ate there. The canteen had multiple purposes, including hosting large group meetings. About a year ago, at Jun's suggestion, the leadership had made an announcement. To keep up the high spirits of the Great Leap Forward

Campaign and to provide a rich life outside work, there would be dance parties at the end of each week.

To prepare for this evening, people had moved the long tables and benches to the sides. On the opposite of the serving counters was a podium, a small rectangle area about two feet higher above the floor. There was a standing microphone and three chairs on the podium.

People dropped in as the day grew darker. Three young men sat down on the podium with a violin, a harmonica, and a flute. Bin-Kai got on the podium with a light leap. He had an accordion strapped to his chest. Since the other three were sitting, his standing up made him stick out. His searching gaze swept the dance floor until he spotted Jun, and he beamed.

Jun wore a short-sleeved white shirt with sky-blue polka dots and a pair of navy-blue pants. Bobby pins behind her ears held her hair back. She was smiling and making small talk with various people who were striking up conversations with her. She glanced at the podium and her eyes widened when she saw Bin-Kai with the accordion, smiling at her. Nodding at him politely, she accepted a dance invitation from a young man.

There was non-stop music and non-stop dancing—the slow waltz (also known as the slow three-step), fast waltz, slow four-step, fast four-step. Bin-Kai's eyes followed Jun on the floor. She danced gracefully, with light feet and excellent coordination. The slight smile on her face was polite, but sent a clear message that she didn't want to be flirted with

During intermission, Jun was sitting on a bench and chatting with two ladies when one of them motioned for her to look up. In front of her, Bin-Kai stood like a tower, beaming. The full length of his body—all 183 cm (6')—stood straight and rigid, like a brick. His arms looked long and hung past his hips, maybe because his upper body was shorter than his long legs. Wide-shouldered with a long neck, he had the air of a military man rather than an athlete.

She stood up and raised her chin so she could look into his eyes.

"Nice accordion playing. Good choice of songs, especially those Soviet Union songs," Jun complimented him with a polite smile.

"You liked them? Thank you!" Bin-Kai rubbed his hands as if he had nowhere to put them. After a slight pause, he asked, "Would you like to dance with me?"

"Aren't you going to keep playing?"

"No, Lao Kang will play his usual accordion for the rest of the evening, so I can enjoy the dance as well."

Right, Jun remembered Lao Kang used to be the accordion player.

"Sure," Jun said, offering him her right hand.

They danced the fast waltz with ease. Jun didn't have to do much. Bin-Kai's right arm lifted her in the air when making turns to avoid traffic and spun her at a much faster pace than she was used to. He was more skillful than other men and did interesting steps she didn't know. She was glad she could follow his strong lead. *How exciting—no, exhilarating!*

Bin-Kai used his peripheral vision to keep track of the traffic and their location on the dance floor. His focal vision was entirely in Jun. She was so light, even with her tall frame. Her height was perfect for them to dance together. Most women were too short, and he'd have to bend down to hold them. Each micro-expression he detected on her face made him wonder what was on her mind. He had so many questions, but this wasn't the time to ask. He wanted to enjoy every moment that he had an excuse to have his arms around her.

The music ended. Bin-Kai led Jun off the dance floor and over toward the bench where she had been sitting. It was customary that when a man picked up a woman from a particular location, he'd return the woman there after the dance. Jun smiled at him and sat down. She needed to quiet her mind, and her heart, a bit.

Another young man came and extended his hand to Jun. Jun stood up, used her left hand to wipe her forehead slightly, and moved onto the dance floor with the man.

When that number was over, she walked back toward her spot and found Bin-Kai sitting there.

So, he must have skipped the last dance, Jun thought.

He stood up and faced her in such a way that no other man could get close to her. For the rest of the dance party, Bin-Kai danced all the dances with Jun. They hardly talked while dancing, which was normal. They did chitchat during the brief breaks. At a certain point in the evening, Bin-Kai stopped returning Jun to her spot, but just continued holding her hand, ready for the next dance.

Bin-Kai was paying full attention to Jun and made sure she was doing the same.

20

GOODBYE

On the bus to Yanshao's place, Jun's mind was busy replaying the dance party again and again, from the moment the party started to the moment she said good night twice to Bin-Kai when he offered to walk her back to her dormitory. She'd had such an exciting evening. She couldn't remember the last time she'd experienced this sensation, if ever.

Yanshao came to the bus station to pick Jun up. There were the familiar smiling faces and understanding gazes between them, and the usual, "How was the ride?" from Yanshao and "It was fine" from Jun. Yanshao carried both bags and Jun walked next to him empty-handed. Five minutes later, they arrived at the place where Yanshao and his mom lived.

Yanshao's mom gave Jun a small smile, took the goodies bag from Yanshao, and examined its contents. "It's so kind of you to always bring goodies. Now rest and have some tea while I'm cooking." She stored most of the tasty treats away and went to the hallway that functioned as a kitchen.

The small two-story building was the tallest one in the neighborhood and the only brick building. Its red color made it stand out even more. The first floor was an office for the town and a room for another bachelor. Yanshao and his mom lived on the second floor. From their windows, one could see several irregular buildings built with mud bricks, a mountain range at a distance, and a vast grassland that extended to the edge of the blue sky.

Yanshao's job was simple—to monitor the water level of a nearby dam and write routine reports. Since there were few educated people, he also helped with various jobs in the town office, such as writing many types of reports, filing files, meeting officers who visited the area, etc. He often complained this was a waste of his education and he didn't see any future in this job.

"Did anyone answer your transfer application?" Jun asked. It was one of the perennial topics between them.

"No. I knew it would be hard because I don't have a good reason to transfer."

The government controlled all jobs centrally. One could change jobs only if the government sent a transfer order.

"Maybe your mom should have stayed in Chifeng so you could use 'taking care of aging mom' to transfer out of here." Jun helped with the brainstorming. With his mom living with him, Yanshao couldn't leave the place for more than a couple of days.

"You know it won't work. Personal reasons are the least important reasons to them, and they'll only agree if they believe the transfer is beneficial to the government, too. Plus, they would suggest bring my mom to live with me."

In moments like this, Jun was grateful she wasn't in a similar place or doing a similar job, even though the salary was the same. If they had requested to be together for job placement, they might have ended up at an even more remote location where there was no civilization, like Ouyang and Fanghua.

Visiting Yanshao was a struggle on several levels. The bumpy bus ride didn't even count for Jun. She'd always felt Yanshao's mom wasn't fond of her and had never warmed up to her. Not having Mama while growing up, Jun hadn't known what to do to please Yanshao's mom beyond her usual friendly manner. When she brought up the concern, Yanshao brushed it aside. "It's not true. She's like that, not showing much affection. If she didn't like you, I'd stop seeing you. You know I won't do anything to hurt her." It did not completely reassure Jun.

Another struggle was the basic living conditions. Growing up, Jun hadn't minded a poor and simple life. But this place was worse than the school life Jun and Xia had. Yanshao would say, "At least this is a town, however small. We have one store open two days a week where we get our living supplies." He admitted, however, that it was boring and lonely. There were no similar-minded people to talk to or engage with. Apart from work, he spent his time reading any books he could get hold of, writing letters to Jun, and running outside if the weather permitted. There was no place to play basketball—no court and not even a flat enough spot.

During her visits, Jun would sleep in Yanshao's single wood bed, near his mom's, and Yanshao would sleep in the office downstairs. Yanshao's mom complained often, saying, "The wood bed is not the same. I miss my warm kang."

As usual, Jun's excitement before the visit turned to depression during it. Besides making and sharing meals, there was little to do. The weather was still nice outside, and they took a daily walk for about 30 minutes. Jun started talking about her last project. When she noticed Yanshao listening silently with a blank face, she skimmed the rest of it because she knew it only made Yanshao regret his job. Yanshao mentioned the books he'd recently read. But Jun couldn't respond because she didn't read them and she wasn't interested either. Jun didn't think it'd be appropriate to talk about the dance party. What to tell him? How would it make him feel? She didn't want to talk about any activities she set up and carried out at work because all those things would only remind Yanshao he had no social life here. Yanshao asked about Xia. Jun's answer took less than a minute because she had little to report.

By the last day of the visit, Jun felt relieved she was about to go back to her own life.

"Come, breakfast is ready. Better have a full stomach before getting on the bus." Yanshao's mom put corn buns and a pot of millet gruel on the table. Yanshao brought empty bowls, chopsticks, and some preserved vegetables. They ate silently.

Jun watched Yanshao. His back was bent as if he'd been defeated in a battle. He lacked the energetic youth of his school years and his spirit was fading, making him look tired and old.

Jun's heart ached for him. Who could blame him? Life had been unfair to him.

Jun felt distressed after each visit. This time, it was more pronounced. Countless times, she had asked what could and would happen between them. The only way for them to be together would be for her to request a transfer here. But that would be a waste indeed, same as it was a waste for Yanshao to be stuck there. She was doing so well and contributing so much to work now. She considered her work as a way to pay back what the government had spent educating her at the vocational school. If she was to come here, what would she do? The talents and training Yanshao had were of no use here, so there would be nothing for her to do either. She couldn't see any future in this place for her career, her personal life, or her future children.

He's the first boy I ever liked. He was there for me and Xia. And he sacrificed his job prospects to be close to me. I wish things could be different. I wish we weren't drifting apart. Lao-Tian-Ye, please help him and his mom!

With a heavy heart, she knew this would be her last visit.

That night, she had a dream. In it, Yanshao was climbing up a tall ladder that seemed to reach into the clouds, and she was right behind him on the ladder. But she lost her footing and her grip. She lost control of her body. She looked down and couldn't see the rest of the ladder, but saw they were high in the air and the ground was far away. Panting, she shouted, "Wait for me, wait!" But her voice made no sound. He continued climbing. She struggled to hold her tangling body still and desperately swung her feet, trying to find the ladder's rungs. But the hand that still held the ladder was getting tired, and she was about to fall from the ladder altogether.

"No! No! Don't let me fall!" she yelled out and woke up.

Jun gasped for breath. Her heart was pounding, and her body was rigid. Realizing it was a dream, she stayed still and stared at the ceiling, letting the physical sensation pass. Her mind was busy and buzzy.

I'm fine. It was just a dream. Mama said dreams were the opposite of reality. I'm fine. I'll be fine.

But she couldn't fall back asleep that night.

What she didn't know at the time were the countless sleepless nights and nightmares in her future. She wouldn't easily forget Yanshao.

21

COURTING

Tump—Tump—Tump.

Solid footsteps on the stairs reached Jun's room on the second floor.

"I'd better get out now. The prince is here again. But isn't it too early? It's only 7 AM." Mimi teased and checked the alarm clock on the desk.

"You needn't go away. He's taking me out for breakfast in the old town. Then we'll go to People's Park." Jun glanced at herself in the small mirror on the wall. Her hair was neat, and her cheeks were rosy, reflecting her excited heart.

"Lucky you! The rest of us barely have enough to fill our stomachs." Mimi teased again.

In the summer of 1962, the entire country was at the tail end of the Great Famine period, which had begun in 1959. Because of the unrealistic goals and practices of the Great Leap Forward Campaign in 1958, many people, especially those in marginal or rural areas, died of starvation.

The institute did its best to provide for its employees. It allowed each person to buy meal tickets for the canteen. Refined and tasty food cost more, such as meals based on wheat flour, rice, millet, and any meat or fish; less tasty food cost less, such as meals made from corn, yam, sorghum rice, and rice husk. Most people didn't have enough food, even the less desirable kind. Jun had always eaten small portions, but her meal tickets were still barely enough. Having a meal outside was a luxury people could only dream of.

Yesterday was the salary pickup day. Bin-Kai once said people should live more and enjoy life a little. Jun thought it was an interesting idea, although she questioned whether Bin-Kai had gone through harsh times growing up, when money was all-important. But Jun appreciated Bin-Kai's gesture of showering her with such luxuries and treats.

Right after Mimi spoke, came the knock on the door. The usual "tap tap tap... tap tap."

Almost daily, Bin-Kai would come to accompany Jun to the canteen to get dinner and bring it back to her room to eat. At dance parties, Bin-Kai would make sure Jun danced with him and only him during the second half when he could dance. These were the best public announcements: He was courting her. Jun didn't object to any of this.

While she'd been away at remote projects, the institute had recruited ten graduates from Tsinghua University, a much higher number than the regular two per year. All of them were men, and Bin-Kai was one of them. As soon as they arrived, people gave Bin-Kai the nickname "The Prince." It wasn't only ladies who voted on the name. Many men agreed the name perfectly described him and his holistic handsomeness.

On the outside, Jun seemed like her regular self, not too eager and not too uninterested as she went along with Bin-Kai's courtship. But on the inside, she was happy and proud to have gained Bin-Kai's attention in such a passionate way. By contrast, Yanshao had always been very mild or only implied he liked her. He had never made a grand gesture to tell the world about their relationship. It was why many of her peers in the middle school and the vocational school didn't realize for such a long time. Maybe Yanshao hadn't wanted to cause a scene. Maybe he hadn't wanted Jun to become public enemy number one to the other girls. Or maybe it had just not been his style to draw attention to such things. Looking back, Jun realized Yanshao had never shown any thunderstorm-style passion for anything toward her. He had always been calm, mature, and mild. Yes, mild.

Jun felt a hand crushing her heart whenever Yanshao popped up in her mind, which was often. The guilt cast a shadow over her time with Bin-Kai sometimes. Bin-Kai would grow concerned when Jun's face turned from sunshine into a dark cloud in a second. "Are you not well?" he'd ask. Jun would take a deep breath and shake her head as if to push those thoughts away.

Today was Sunday, the one day off from work. Bin-Kai crossed his long leg over a bike he borrowed from a coworker yesterday, held the bike with his feet, and waited for Jun to sit in the backseat. He pedaled to the old town of Hohhot.

Despite being the capital of the Inner Mongolia region, most of Hohhot's population was Han, and they lived and worked in the new town that had developed rapidly since 1947, when Inner Mongolia became an official autonomous region. The old town section had various ethnic and religious minorities, including Mongols, Muslims, and Mans. They preserved their cultures, crafts, and food. One could find many authentic and affordable ethnic dishes there.

Bin-Kai ordered Mongol milk tea and Hohhot shaomai, the most famous breakfast in Hohhot. Ever since he discovered shaomai, which differed from the same-named food he'd had elsewhere, Bin-Kai would find all kinds of excuses to have them. A type of dumpling, the Hohhot shaomai had a paper-thin wrap with minced mutton, ginger, and scallion inside, and was steamed to perfection.

After breakfast, they rode to the People's Park. It was in the central location between the new and the old towns. The artificially created park had a vast lake, several smaller ponds, many curvy pathways, and many benches under big willow trees by the water. For four months of the cold and long winter, people could ice skate on the lake. In the summer, vegetation and annual flowers were abundant. With the warm weather, the lake was open for rowboat rentals.

Bin-Kai led Jun to the rental booth.

"I can't swim," Jun hesitated.

"Don't worry. I'll rescue you if necessary. But these are very safe boats and won't tip over. See, over there, there are kids on them and they're laughing and moving." Bin-Kai pointed to two boats out on the lake.

Jun smiled. The thought of being rescued made her heart pound.

The supposed one-hour rowing adventure became a three-hour one. They chatted about co-workers, work experience, and swapped stories from their school days and childhood. It was a smooth conversation, nothing forced, and no pretending. They rowed to various corners of the lake, then parked in the shade of an enormous willow tree. Jun extended her arm to pull a hanging branch and examine the leaves on it. Bin-Kai admired her graceful movements.

He put the oars down and asked, "Any plans for the Moon Festival?"

Jun paused for a moment. She hadn't thought about it. Work and organizing social activities had kept her busy. "Not yet," she replied. "How about you?"

"I want to visit my family for a couple of days. I haven't seen them since the Spring Festival."

"Do you see them often?"

"As much as I can."

"Tell me more about your family."

"I've told you a lot. What else do you need to know?"

Bin-Kai laughed. For someone who talked little, he couldn't believe how much he'd shared with her about his family. He was surprised by how much he admired and adored Jun. Sure, her appearance was what had first gotten his attention. But over time, he learned there was so much to love beyond Jun's beauty. She was a modern woman with an excellent education and had a life of her own. She could carry herself in tough situations, such as remote work environments. Not only did she do these things as easily as breathing air, but she did them exceptionally well. She was a leader among young people and helped to make her peers feel at home in the institute. His ears were full of praise for Jun. People liked to gossip, and men liked to talk or tease about single women in the institute, but so far, he had heard nothing negative about her. Being associated with her made him proud and made him want to be a better version of himself.

Bin-Kai thought about his parents. They had a deep affection for each other. But his father never had conversations with his mom like he had with Jun. His mom was bright too, but was limited to her own world of being a stay-at-home parent, whereas Jun was his equal. He could sense a deep intellectual connection with her, which was rare and precious to him.

Bin-Kai grinned at Jun and said, "Okay. Ask one more question about my family. No, ask as many as you want. Tell me what you want to know."

Jun recalled what Bin-Kai had told her about his family and said, "It's so sad your parents lost a baby girl."

"I know. After four boys, my parents wanted a girl badly, especially my mom. It didn't happen. Any more questions?"

Jun shook her head. She couldn't think of another question to ask.

Bin-Kai looked at Jun intensely and said, "I'd like to take you to meet them for the Moon Festival."

This was as official as a marriage proposal.

"I'm... are you sure?" Jun's stomach tightened with the loaded surprise. It had only been nine months since they first met, and among those nine months, he'd been away for six. Plus, she hadn't officially said goodbye to Yanshao, although their lack of seeing each other and less frequent letters might represent an unspoken breakup.

"I'm sure. What's your reason not to go to see them?" Bin-Kai asked.

Reasons? Jun could think of several. But she didn't vocalize them and concealed any related emotions from her face. She ran through them in her head.

What if Bin-Kai's family wasn't fond of me? Jun still thought it was the case with Yanshao's mom. Otherwise, they might have been together by now... or would they?

What if accepting Bin-Kai's invitation would hurt Yanshao because it meant our relationship ended? But did they have a relationship at all? They had gone to the same middle school and vocational school, and they'd spent more time together than either had with anyone else of the opposite gender. But they had never openly stated their relationship to the public or themselves. It was all assumed. If they had a relationship, why were they not married yet? Counting on her fingers, they'd known each other for eight years. He'd never brought up marriage. Did he intend to marry her? He must. Otherwise, why would he choose an inferior job to be closer to her?

But if Yanshao intended to marry me, he'd better hurry. She was 26, and he was 25, not young anymore.

What if Yanshao and I get married? What kind of life would it be? Jun wouldn't want to be transferred to his place. They'd live separately as married singles, like Mimi. They'd wait for the chance he might get a job transfer, which could never happen. They wouldn't have a home if they weren't living together, and it would be hard to have children in such a situation.

Hadn't our relationship ended already? Neither of them said goodbye, but both of them had shown it. The last time Jun received a letter from Yanshao had been several months ago, right before the Spring Festival, and Yanshao never wrote back after she responded. She knew her letter had been short and boring because she couldn't find more interesting things to write about.

Now in front of me is this handsome and available Tsinghua graduate who seemed so eager to claim me as his. Things he did made her heart race. She wanted to see him, talk with him, and do things together with him. He made her feel loved, wanted, and important. Each day they spent together was like a warm summer's day for her. They could have a future together. There couldn't be a better arrangement than working at the same institute. They would have an apartment designated for married people in the institute. Their kids would go to the daycare and the elementary school hosted by the institute.

But do I know him enough? They had only spent time together in person for roughly three months. So far, all was rosy and positive, and she had detected no faults in him. And of course, he hadn't detected any in her either.

Maybe the trip would be a wonderful opportunity to get to know him better? Yes, it would be a sensible and good enough reason—to get to know him better.

I can always vocalize my unwillingness to move forward if I change my mind.

Jun pulled her mind back to the here and now. "Have you told your family about me?"

"Not yet, but I'll write to them tonight if you agree to go. Say yes, please."

"Yes, I'll go with you to meet your family."

22

ZHOU FAMILY

Bin-Kai's father, Mr. Zhou, was born in 1914 in Jinzhou, a major city in the northeast. His parents owned land and hired workers, and they provided Mr. Zhou with four years of private education. In 1940, at age 26, Mr. Zhou found a business partner and set up a factory for wheat flour processing. Wheat flour was and is a major food source for people in northern China. With the success of the business, in 1946, he and his business partner established another facility in Shenyang, a bigger and more central city, about 225 km (140 miles) away from Jinzhou. To accommodate the size and demand of the second factory, they built train tracks inside the workshops, allowing finished products to reach distant destinations.

The two plants were prosperous despite the turbulence of the Civil War. In 1949, the People's Liberation Army (PLA) won the war, and the Communist Party became the ruling party of the new China. Because of the strategic importance of the facility in Shenyang, the government seized it.

The 1951–1952 Three-Anti and Five-Anti Campaigns targeted allegedly corrupt officials, government bureaucrats, capitalists, and business owners. Since Mr. Zhou was the richest person in Jinzhou, owning a business and a vast house, the government classified him as a "Capitalist" and sent him to a re-education camp. These camps reformed criminals and the lowest-class people through physical labor. Mr. Zhou showed remorse and good behavior and came out eight months later, four months sooner than scheduled. He continued managing the Jinzhou plant. His capitalist classification became the family class and affected all members of future generations.

In 1956, during the Joint State–Private Ownership Movement, Mr. Zhou's Jinzhou plant became a workshop for a state-owned facility. Leadership in merged businesses like these included both government officials and private property owners. Representing the latter, Mr. Zhou became the manager of this workshop. Soon after, he received a promotion to the position of vice president. Two years later, he took on the role of a manager in a major wheat warehouse in Jinzhou.

Mr. Zhou's quick wit, open-mindedness, and generous nature, as well as his handsome looks, tall frame (175 cm or 5'9"), and magnificent manners, made him a well-liked and highly respected figure in the local community.

Mr. Zhou's wife was born in the same place as Mr. Zhou. Her nickname was Lao-Si, meaning the fourth child of the family. She had two older brothers and an older sister, and a younger brother and sister. The old norm would have considered her to be a well-rounded and perfect child who had every type of family relations: both parents, older brothers and sisters, and younger brothers and sisters. Because of this, people invited her to represent perfection and luck at various ceremonies. Her parents owned land but only hired workers at busy times. Their family class was "Middle Peasants." In the tradition of reputable families, the parents bound all three sisters' feet when they were a few months old, resulting in their feet being only three inches long when fully grown. The girls received no education and couldn't read or write. This was typical. Most families did not care to educate their daughters because, upon marriage, they would belong to their husbands' families.

Parents arranged marriages and people wed at a young age. Mr. Zhou's wife was three years older than him. This was a desirable situation in a marriage, according to an old saying: "A three-years-older wife ensures a prosperous life."

After being married, Lao-Si's name on Zhou's family tree became a combination of her husband's and her father's last names, plus a character showing she was a married woman. Elder neighbors and friends still called her "Lao-Si." People from the same generation called her "Sister Si." And the younger generation called her "Aunt Si." She had no identity or duties other than raising children and taking care of domestic chores. Despite the old notion that "A married daughter is like splashed water," and despite being a middle child, Lao-Si maintained an excellent reputation in her parents' large and extended family and among their neighbors and friends. She had a powerful mind and many great ideas. Marrying a rich and influential man also helped boost her reputation, and she continued to be highly sought after in many situations.

During the Great Leap Forward Campaign from 1958 to 1960, Mr. Zhou had limited income and struggled to support their two older sons in college while also raising two younger sons, aged 10 and

16. Although they sold some eggs and Lao-Si sewed to earn money, the financial hole was still too big.

"Maybe I should find a job," Lao-Si mentioned one day after dinner.

"No way. You never worked in your whole life. I don't want you to work now." Mr. Zhou protested.

"That was true in the old days. But we have to face reality. Our sons eat so much because they're growing. We have to make sure Bin-Kai can finish college. He desperately needs a new pair of shoes. And we haven't seen him for a year. He has no money to buy a train ticket."

Mr. Zhou was silent. A sense of shame came over him—he felt inadequate as a husband and as the head of the household.

Lao-Si glanced at him. "It's not your fault. There are so many things we have no control over. We just need to cope."

"I'll see what jobs I can find for you." Out of desperation for the situation and knowing his wife's stubbornness, Mr. Zhou yielded.

Lao-Si joined a plant that produced preserved vegetables. Such vegetables were household commodities given the short growing seasons and the need to preserve crops. For the first time, she was required to have a formal name to identify her.

"Oh well, may as well recognize my family's name," Lao-Si teased. Working women, even if married, kept their family names. Only traditional and stay-at-home married women inherited their husbands' family names.

Lao-Si, or Yu Shanglan—Mr. Zhou helped her with the official name—worked six hours per day, six days per week. The salary was handsome and wasn't based on education level or experience. The assembly line, however, was brutal to Lao-Si. Workers had to stand and could only rest periodically for a short period. Lao-Si's feet hurt badly. On the first day, she persevered at work but collapsed at home after Mr. Zhou carried her home on a bike.

"Lay in bed. I'll take your shoes off." Mr. Zhou helped Lao-Si to the kang. He tried to remove her shoes, but they had gotten stuck to her swollen feet. Blood came out around the edges of the shoes and her entire lower legs were swollen. Mr. Zhou fetched a pair of scissors and cut off her shoes.

Lao-Si was too tired to protest about how much money and time it would cost to make another pair of shoes.

Gently massaging Lao-Si's feet and lower legs with salt, Mr. Zhou made sure Lao-Si couldn't see his tears.

"This is madness. You won't go back tomorrow." Mr. Zhou said in a low voice.

"The beginning is hard. It'll get better. Tomorrow, I'll bring a pair of old shoes from our son's early days and put them on during work. It'll be fine."

Two years had gone by. Lao-Si was doing fine at work and proudly brought home money comparable to what her husband earned.

One day, a lady named Bohua, who worked next to her, fainted and collapsed on the floor. Lao-Si knew Bohua was pregnant even though it didn't show yet. The next day, a new lady was in Bohua's place.

"Are you a filler or a permanent worker?" asked Lao-Si.

"Oh, I'm hired for a permanent position." The new lady said proudly.

They must have fired Bohua because of her pregnancy. Lao-Si bit into her lips.

When the floor manager did the regular inspection routine, Lao-Si couldn't help herself. "It's not fair you let Bohua go. Bohua is a great worker. She could still work a few more months until, well, until her pregnancy shows or until she couldn't work."

The manager looked at Lao-Si with irritation. "She fainted and couldn't work! Many people want jobs, and many can replace her. We have to produce. It was a business decision, not a personal one."

"But ..." Lao-Si was searching for the right words.

"She would have to leave eventually, anyway," the manager said.

Lao-Si sighed. "Bohua is very kind and has covered me and others many times."

"You'd better watch yourself. This isn't the first time you've caused a stir," the manager snapped, giving Lao-Si a sharp stare.

Lao-Si made a scornful sound and continued her work, but it was the last day of her working career.

Fortunately, by then, the oldest son, Bin-Kai, had graduated from college and started a job. One of the two younger ones had graduated from middle school and found a job as a railroad conductor.

Their second son, Bin-Long, was born in 1937, two years younger than Bin-Kai. Binlong preferred staying inside and at home over any activities happening in the family, school, or neighborhood. So much so that his 195 cm (6'4") frame was hardly ever seen by anyone outside the family, as if he didn't exist. Attending college and working in a faraway city as a mechanical engineer suited him well. The family only saw him once or twice a year. Lao-Si was always worried about his heart condition.

"Ever since he was a little boy, his heart has been weak. Why did he turn out to be this tall? Much harder on his heart! And why does he live so far? Who will take care of him if anything happens to him?" Lao-Si complained many times.

Bin-Nan would often comfort his mom in these moments. "Don't worry, Ma. Giant can take care of himself." The boys had nicknamed Binlong Giant.

Born in 1942, Bin-Nan was the shortest of all the sons, which earned him the nickname Shorty. His height seemed to confirm the old saying that brain development takes up all the energy meant for physical growth. He was the go-to person for any problems. Not only did he have witty ideas, but he was warm and caring and often made people feel good. He never thought about leaving his family and going somewhere else for school or work. To ease the family's financial burden, he chose to become a railroad conductor as soon as he graduated from middle school.

The fourth son, Bin-Pei, was born in 1948, and soon earned for himself the nickname Naughty. At a young age, Bin-Pei was fearless, wild, and engaged in dangerous behavior. He received many complaints from his school. He caused headaches not only for his parents but for his brothers too.

Lao-Si could handle whatever challenges and troubles her sons brought. What had eaten her heart up all these years was the loss of her baby girl. Two years after Bin-Pei was born, Lao-Si had given birth to a girl, and this had filled Lao-Si's heart with joy, and filled her mind with the notion of "perfection" she had maintained all her life—having children of all genders.

Unfortunately, the baby girl got sick before she'd turned three months old. A few days later, she passed away. They never learned what the illness was that had caused her death. A part of Lao-Si's heart had died with the girl. She packed the baby girl's clothes and buried them at the bottom of the clothing chest. She hoped another girl might come into their life again, but it wasn't to be—in the end, they had only sons.

23

FUTURE IN-LAWS

The Moon Festival, also called the Mid-Autumn Festival, has been one of the biggest holidays. At harvest time, there's often abundant food and goodies during the celebration.

Two days before the Moon Festival in 1962, Jun and Bin-Kai took an overnight train for fourteen hours from Hohhot to Beijing and another train for eight hours to Jinzhou. It seemed to Jun like Jinzhou was just about as far away from Hohhot as her hometown was. Sadly, her hometown wasn't worth visiting anymore, as her entire family had left the city by this point.

Upon arrival at Jinzhou train station, Bin-Kai hired a rickshaw to carry the two of them and a few pieces of luggage to his family's home.

Shorty Bin-Nan and Naughty Bin-Pei were waiting at the gate.

"Welcome—we've been expecting you," Bin-Nan said with a grin and unloaded the luggage.

Bin-Pei jumped up and down with one hand holding an ear of corn. "We bought lots of yummy food!" he exclaimed with his mouth full.

Bin-Kai patted his back and said, "Are you still eating non-stop? Well, you must need it, you're growing. Help Shorty take the luggage inside."

Bin-Kai turned his face to Jun with a tilt of his head. "Let's go meet my parents." He led the way, and Jun followed.

The courtyard was deep and surrounded on all four sides by different areas of the homestead. It reminded Jun of the home her father had built, their small mansion with houses on four sides. Here, though, the house sat on the north side and had three rooms. One side of the yard had a large pig run with two pigs in it. The other side had a shed for storage and a chicken coop. Over ten chickens were running loose in the yard. The gate side comprised just a wall. Bin-Kai told her their original house had been much bigger, but they'd had to move to this house after Mr. Zhou donated their house as a gesture of remorse during his re-education.

Bin-Kai and Jun stepped into the entry room. It connected the east and west rooms and served as the kitchen. A tall table had stools under it, and two cooking stoves led to each of the two rooms on either side, to heat the kangs in those rooms.

Bin-Kai stood by the opened door of the west room and gestured for Jun to enter.

Mr. Zhou was sitting on the edge of the big kang that took up half of the room on the south side. A kang table, about 3 feet by 3 feet and 1 foot high, was close to the edge of the kang, and two teacups and one teapot were on it. Mr. Zhou's right elbow landed on the kang table, and his legs dangled on the kang. He was wearing a black formal Chinese suit for men, the white shirt collar showing at his neckline. His big black eyes looked out from beneath dark, heavy eyebrows. He had a neat haircut, a straight back, and an air of authority and intelligence. He looked much younger than 47.

Lao-Si was sitting on the other side of the kang table, a piece of cloth in one hand and a needle in another. Her hair was in a low bun. Her crossed legs hid her feet. As they entered, she straightened her back and looked up. Her eyes were narrow, her face pale, and her cheeks loose. She could easily have been mistaken as Mr. Zhou's mother.

Bin-Kai said, "Ma, Ba, this is Liu Jun."

Mr. Zhou and Lao-Si both sat there without moving. They looked Jun up and down.

Jun was uncomfortable. This reminded her of the moments when matchmakers had brought in young girls for her two brothers. People examined these girls as if they were objects of potential value. She never imagined she would find herself in that position, but here she was, being examined just like they had been.

Of course, this makes sense. This family seems like a traditional family, like my family, even though times have changed.

Her reasoning made her more at ease. She opened her mouth, and after a slight hesitation, said, "Uncle Zhou, Aunt Yu, how are you?"

Mr. Zhou and Lao-Si were both taken aback. Too late, Jun remembered traditional families believed girls shouldn't speak unless someone had asked them a question.

Oh, well. I'm not an uneducated girl whose only value is to give birth to family heirs and do chores. I'm educated and an intellectual and I earn a salary. She smiled.

"We're good. How nice of you to visit," Mr. Zhou broke the silence and nodded at Jun. "Come and sit on the kang. You must be tired after the long trip." He stepped down from the kang and offered a place for Jun on his side of the kang table.

Jun was, in fact, tired. Her back hurt a little, and she was thirsty.

"Bin-Nan, bring teacups!" Mr. Zhou called.

"Coming!" Bin-Nan flew in with light feet. He grinned at Jun and put two teacups on the kang table, filled them with hot tea from the teapot, and exited the room. Jun heard him saying to Naughty, "She's so pretty!"

Jun sat at the kang table and drank the tea without talking. She sensed Lao-Si watching her the whole time.

After finishing the tea in the cup, Lao-Si said, "There's more tea in the pot. Fill it yourself."

Jun was relieved Lao-Si had spoken, and in a tone that wasn't too cold, although it wasn't warm either.

Jun filled the teacup and asked, "Is that a shirt you're sewing?"

"This is a shirt for Bin-Pei. He always needs new clothes. Can you sew?"

"Yes, I do all the sewing and shoemaking for myself and my sister."

Lao-Si glanced at Jun. "Can you cook?"

"Oh. I've only cooked for two or three people. We used to have someone who cooked at home when my family was large and I was young. But later, my sister and I lived in a schoolroom. We had simple meals. I've eaten in the canteen, both at school and work." Jun thought about her mom, who for a while had cooked three meals a day for the family. She sighed inwardly.

"You won't be eating in the canteen once you're married. We cook our meals. That's what families do." Lao-Si said in a matter-of-fact tone.

"Our married colleagues eat in the canteen, too. Cooking takes time and costs more money than eating in the canteen." Jun answered, realizing she might have talked too much.

There was a long pause.

Mr. Zhou asked, "Will you quit your job after getting married? It is our custom that the eldest son's wife lives with her in-laws."

"What? No." Jun was caught off guard by the question and burst out the words without thinking. She'd never thought about quitting her job, which she had worked so hard for, and associated her identity with. She never planned to be a stay-home mom, or she'd be married long ago. They didn't know how good she was at her work, and how much respect she earned from her colleagues. She thought about her brothers' wives and how her parents had had similar expectations as Bin-Kai's parents.

Mr. Zhou stood up and went outside. Lao-Si was silent.

Jun looked around. *When did Bin-Kai leave the room?* She couldn't think of anything else to say. She kept sipping tea.

Mr. Zhou came in and said, "Dinner's ready."

Lao-Si put down her sewing, used her hands to scoot to the edge of the kang, then used a small stepstool to descend to the floor with her 3-inch feet. She was slightly shorter than Jun, but her straight back and long neck made her look tall. She walked smoothly and steadily, although only a few inches at a time. If someone were to see only her upper body, they wouldn't be able to tell she had such small feet.

Jun followed Lao-Si out to the kitchen.

The six of them sat at the tall table with roasted pork, steamed fish, stir-fried vegetables, and steamed buns. All the food was familiar to Jun. She heard her stomach growling and was eager to pick up the chopsticks, but she knew she'd have to wait until after the elder ones started. After Mr. Zhou and Lao-Si picked up their chopsticks, Bin-Kai picked up a bite from each dish and put it in her bowl.

They finished dinner in silence. Jun learned it was their family rule that no one should talk when eating, and people should not talk with their mouth full.

At night, Bin-Nan and Bin-Pei went back to the west room to sleep in the big kang with their parents and Bin-Kai. Jun slept in the east room by herself.

Over the next two days, Bin-Kai showed Jun around the town. It was bigger than Chifeng and had similar street scenes, stores, and food.

On the evening before Bin-Kai and Jun were to leave, Mr. Zhou said to Bin-Kai, "We need to talk." They went to the west room. Lao-Si was there, sitting on the kang as usual.

Bin-Kai had expected this talk. After all, he had brought Jun home to let his parents know his intentions.

Lao-Si started, "Jun is a pretty girl. But she may not be a good fit for you or our family. She has no family values and doesn't know traditional customs."

"What do you mean?" asked Bin-Kai.

"A girl from a family of wealth and status would have known to decline your father's offer to take his seat. She'd either stand or sit in the chair by the corner—not on the kang by the table when an elder is there already. She should know her position of being a youngster."

"But Ba offered it. It would have been rude to decline."

Lao-Si shot Bin-Kai a sharp glance and continued. "She talks to us as if we're her peers, not her elders. A good parent should have taught her those customs. But then, she grew up without parents."

"She grew up in a different city, in an unusual situation. Plus, she could learn these customs in no time. She's very smart and well-educated," Bin-Kai said quietly.

"A daughter-in-law doesn't need to be smart or educated," Lao-Si declared.

"But Ma, we're in a new time now. You didn't go to school, but more women have the opportunity now, and Jun was an outstanding student. That's why she works alongside me in the same institute."

Mr. Zhou said, "She said she doesn't plan to quit her job and live with us after being married."

"We haven't talked about it yet. But if she doesn't quit, I don't see why that would be a problem. We'd live and work together. She earns a good salary. Two incomes help."

Mr. Zhou nodded. "It's a different time for sure. Two incomes help. Your Ma had to work in the factory when you were in college. Having regular-sized feet helps too. Your Ma had to quit her job because she couldn't stand for long enough." Mr. Zhou didn't want to disclose that Lao-Si had been fired.

"So, you agree she can keep her job after marriage?" Bin-Kai was excited.

Mr. Zhou was thoughtful. "There's something about this girl I'm not sure about. Growing up with no parents is not necessarily a concern. She seems very independent and strong-willed. Those could be good qualities, depending on the situation."

"You don't know her well," Bin-Kai said, feeling hopeful.

"There are certain things you know right away," returned Mr. Zhou.

Bin-Kai was silent. He didn't always take his mom's reasoning seriously, but he respected and trusted his father. He could see why his father had had a successful business career.

But his father couldn't nail down his concerns about Jun. It cast a shadow over Bin-Kai's heart. He wished the letter he'd sent them before the visit had contained more details to prepare them to accept Jun as a woman of the new generation. But like his father, he wasn't good at words, let alone lengthy letters. He hoped that with time, Jun could earn his parents' approval. After all, they were reasonable people.

***

On the train back from Jinzhou, Jun reflected on the visit with Bin-Kai.

"Your two brothers are fine boys," she observed.

"Aren't they? They adore you," said Bin-Kai.

Jun nodded. She'd overheard them more than once talking about her favorably.

"I think Shorty Bin-Nan is very brainy. Too bad your family business doesn't exist anymore. Bin-Nan would have been a great successor to your father. He's the one who should eventually take over the family affairs, for sure."

"Good observation. What about Naughty?"

"He's almost the opposite of Shorty. He'd be a good follower, but if he follows the wrong person, it could be dangerous."

"I agree. Too bad you didn't get to meet Giant. But what about me? The big brother among all?" Bin-Kai teased, smiling at Jun.

Jun thought it was interesting that, just like in her own family, the eldest son had decided not to be a businessperson and instead went far away from the family. Bin-Kai was too rigorous for business—he was highly intelligent, yet his social skills were lacking. But she didn't want to point that weakness out.

"You're good at what you do as a civil engineer and you're a good big brother! It's obvious you're very close to your family, with all the frequent visits and keeping up to date with what your younger brothers are up to."

Jun paused, thinking about her own big brothers. She wished Xi-Chang would be more caring toward her and Xia. She sensed Xi-Chang loved her and Xia in a brotherly way, but he didn't seem to know how to show more affection. Maybe because he'd been such a young boy when he left home and hadn't spent a lot of time around family members. Even though they had finally reconnected, she rarely received a letter from him and last saw him more than a year ago when she'd taken a three-day vacation to visit him.

Jun also thought about her second brother, Xi-Dan, who was even more distant. Xia was the only sibling Jun was close to. Fortunately, they were geographically close and could see each other more often—usually when Xia came to visit her.

Jun reflected on Mr. Zhou.

"Your father is extremely handsome and seems highly intelligent, with good social skills. He spoke little, but what he said was on point and impeccable. Of course, he manages thousands of people as a founder and director of major flour processing plants. I can only imagine he must have been even more attractive when he was young."

"More handsome than me?" Bin-Kai raised an eyebrow and made a funny face.

"I can see where you got your good looks." Jun tapped his chin dimple.

She thought Mr. Zhou had been civil toward her and seemed fond of her. She couldn't think of anything he'd said or done that would imply he had a low opinion of her. Jun smiled.

"What are you smiling about?" Bin-Kai asked, alert.

"Your father reminds me of my father, though in a different way. I was close to my father; I had so much affection for him and thought highly of him. And I admire your father's good qualities, and I'm growing fond of him."

"Glad to know you're fond of my father. That's important."

Jun wondered what her father would say about the potential marriage to Bin-Kai. She'd listen to him if he were still alive. Jun let out a long exhale. She missed her father.

Lao-Si had made a different impression on Jun. For starters, she was illiterate, with plain looks, and a proud or rude manner. But Mr. Zhou seemed to respect Lao-Si and had a deep affection for her, even though he wasn't an emotionally demonstrative person.

Jun eyed Bin-Kai, whose eyes were closed now as he prepared to settle in for a nap. She hoped she would receive the same respect and affection from Bin-Kai that Mr. Zhou gave Lao-Si. Jun did admire Lao-Si's toughness. It couldn't be easy to never leave the house, raise four sons, many chickens, and two pigs, and attend to her husband. Lao-Si seemed to have no complaints and accepted her life. Her view of the world was narrow, and she expected her daughter-in-law to be like her. If there were any challenges in her relationship with Bin-Kai, Jun foresaw they would come from Lao-Si. Maybe it would end up being just a run-of-the-mill mother–daughter-in-law bitterness? Jun wasn't sure.

She shook her head as if to shake off any negative feelings. Overall, she felt like this trip had been a success. She looked at Bin-Kai's handsome face and smiled to herself. He was a rare find, and their future together would be bright.

Jun closed her eyes and rested her head on Bin-Kai's shoulder.

24

TROUBLES

On Jun's 27th birthday, or at least on the anniversary of the day she thought she'd been born—which was two months after they returned from visiting Bin-Kai's family—Bin-Kai took Jun out to a local diner for dinner. Jun had never been a big fan of birthdays. For one thing, she wasn't sure she'd actually been born on this exact day since her mom had only estimated it based on the Chinese calendar. For another, she couldn't remember ever celebrating anyone's birthday at home. Birthdays just reminded her of the passing of her parents.

But Bin-Kai had been excited about this day ever since he heard Jun accidentally mention it a few days prior. He wanted this outing to be a surprise and hadn't told Jun until he came to her dorm like he usually did to pick her up to go to the canteen.

He took Jun to a place he had been before. After sitting down, he ordered two dishes, too fancy to appear on the menu of the canteen and too greasy for Jun.

When the dishes came, Jun sat there with no appetite.

He picked these dishes without asking me what I wanted to eat. Yanshao would have never done that. He always checked with me first to make sure my needs had been met.

Jun's tears were lingering behind her eyes. She felt neglected.

Bin-Kai also ordered a small pot of liquor and one small shot glass.

"Eat, eat. So much better than the food we usually get." He waved his chopsticks at Jun.

Jun slowly picked up the chopsticks. Not only did she have no appetite, but she also felt nauseous. *It must be the smell of the liquor.*

Bin-Kai had already swallowed a few mouthfuls of the food and a couple of shots of alcohol.

Jun put down her chopsticks. "I'm not hungry."

Bin-Kai looked at her, his mouth busily chewing, and asked, "Not feeling well? Or you don't like the food?"

Jun moved her face away from him to avoid the odor of the alcohol. She wanted to throw up now. She jumped up and ran to the washroom. A few minutes later, she came back to the table.

About two-thirds of the food was gone.

He looked at her as she walked toward the table, finished his mouthful of food, and said with little concern, "Are you alright?"

She sat down on the opposite side of the table, the farthest away from him.

"Why are we here tonight?" she asked, trying to keep her voice even.

"You're turning 27."

"Is this for me?"

"Well, it's a good reason to go out."

"So, it's not for me. No wonder you ordered dishes I don't like."

"I didn't know you didn't like them. We'll get another one you like."

"You didn't even ask me."

Bin-Kai paused and realized it was true.

"You didn't even ask if I like sake or not and you assumed I don't because you only asked for one glass." Jun's voice raised a little.

"Right. Right." He turned to the front counter. "Server, bring another cup."

"I don't drink. I hate alcohol. It makes me sick." Jun said, her face twisting in disgust.

Bin-Kai sat there quietly. He regretted not having been more sensitive to her needs and was disgusted at himself for being so self-centered. Having been single for so long, he wasn't used to considering another person when making decisions. He wished the evening could restart and he could do the whole thing differently. But his pride wouldn't allow him to say anything. He just sat there, stone-faced.

Jun was disappointed. He said nothing and his expression seemed to broadcast, "I don't care." She stood up. "I want to go back now. Sitting here makes me sick. You can finish your meal."

Bin-Kai didn't speak but stood up right away and walked Jun to the door, then back to their singles' building.

***

For the next three days, Jun couldn't keep anything down. Whatever she ate, she'd throw up. She was tired and depressed and had trouble concentrating at work. Bin-Kai hadn't visited her after work as usual. They hadn't seen each other since Jun's birthday.

Mimi brought meals back for her.

"You look so pale and weak. Maybe you should see a doctor. By the way, if you don't plan to touch this food, I'll eat it again." Mimi said.

Jun visited the clinic office of the institute. It was like a nurse's station with one person on staff and medicines for common illnesses.

"Nothing seems wrong. Is your period regular?" asked the nurse.

"It has never been," Jun answered.

"When was the last time you had it?"

Jun calculated. It was weeks before they visited his family.

"To be safe, try this." The nurse gave her a package and led her to the back.

When she returned the package to the nurse, the nurse's face changed.

"Did you know you are pregnant?"

Blood rushed to Jun's head. She was dizzy and lost her balance. The nurse grabbed her before she fell and sat her on a chair.

How could this be? We only did it once. He was so persistent and passionate. He said it would only be a matter of time since I had met his family already. It was so hard to push him away. I should have been firm. How could I do this to myself? What a stupid thing to do.

The nurse brought a cup of hot water. "You can rest on the bench until you can walk."

Jun put all her strength together and stood up. "No, I need to go back to work." She turned to the nurse and added, "You're so kind. Can I ask you a favor?"

The nurse nodded.

"Can you keep this a secret? Please don't tell anyone, I mean anyone."

The nurse nodded again. "There's no reason to tell anyone. I'll write a note so you can request a medical leave for a few days. It will help you regain your strength. You're too weak to walk, let alone work."

In bed, Jun spent her time trying to figure out her next steps. What to do, what to do! She couldn't tell anyone. This wasn't something one could confide in anyone. An unmarried woman getting pregnant? She could think of nothing more shameful. If this news got out, it would forever ruin her reputation. How could she live? How could she keep working here?

No, don't let anyone know. Not even Xia, not even Mimi. No one can know.

Mimi continued helping Jun by bringing meals back to their room and helping with some domestic chores. In return, Mimi received grateful words and saved herself some meal allowance tickets.

"Where's Bin-Kai? Do you want me to bring him to see you?" asked Mimi.

"No. We argued the other day."

Jun realized this had been their first fight, even though she had done all the talking and he had said nothing.

What was with him? Was I right to think of him as selfish and uncaring? Wasn't it a departure from the way he treated me before we visited his family? Yes, it was different. He never ignored me before. Was it because we visited his family and were a presumed couple? Or wait! Was it because... was it because he had already claimed me by... by...

Oh, my headache! My chest pain! My stupidity!

***

Troubles plagued Bin-Kai. He didn't realize how selfish he'd been until Jun had pointed it out. How could he do such a thing? He had acted as if Jun wasn't even there. Since college years, he had gone out to diners by himself about once a year around his birthday. He had done the same thing he'd always done, ordered two dishes and a pot of liquor. He'd done it out of habit. Only now he wasn't alone anymore. He had Jun right there by his side. Plus, they were supposed to be celebrating her birthday. No wonder she was upset. It was the first time he'd seen her upset. It made him feel a bit chilled to the bone to see her get upset. Her eyes had grown large, and her pupils looked as deep as a bottomless well.

What was running through her head? There must be more than what she said. Will she ever forgive me? Will she leave me for someone else? There are plenty of Tsinghua graduates who would leap at the chance. One of them had even said to him the other day, "Bin-Kai, you're the luckiest man on earth. But the moment she leaves you, I'll pursue her with all I've got."

He hadn't seen her in the canteen. She didn't come to the dance party. One day, he used an excuse to deliver a folder to her project team on a different floor and he didn't see her there. He was too proud to ask her teammates about her. He wondered if he should go see her after work as usual. But what if she was still mad at him? Maybe he should give her some time to recover from being upset. Or maybe he could use the excuse of checking if her sickness was gone. But it was too obvious an excuse. Who wouldn't be sickened by a selfish man's behavior?

One week passed before Bin-Kai finally saw Jun in the canteen. He rushed toward her. Standing in front of her, he couldn't believe his eyes. She looked five years older. Her rosy cheeks were now pale. The red lips Bin-Kai loved so much were pink. She walked slowly, a stark contrast to her usual light, brisk steps. Her face was downturned and a shadow lingered in her eyes.

"How have you been?" He asked in a tender tone. At this moment, she was his entire world.

"I'm better now," she answered politely. "I took a few days from work and rested."

Bin-Kai wanted to punch himself.

You were a fool. You made her so sick she had to take medical leave, and you stayed away all this time.

"Did I... Can I do something for you? Can I come to visit you?" He tried to be contained and not show his anguish, so his words came out sounding calm and unaffectionate.

Jun hesitated for a moment. "No. I need more time to rest."

In her mind, she was thinking, *this is his reaction after hearing what I said?* She turned around and walked out of the canteen with her bowl of food.

***

Bin-Kai thought long and hard. He took out his father's letter again to read. It had arrived two days ago. His father hardly ever wrote letters. During the entire five years of college, he'd only received two letters from his father.

In this letter, Mr. Zhou laid out a few reasons and thoughts and suggested it would benefit the Zhou family and Bin-Kai himself if he'd marry a traditional girl whom they had found for him already.

"Your Ma and I know you better than you know yourself. You're old enough now to start a family. Come back and meet her and we can have the wedding during the Spring Festival."

His father only wrote to him when he was trying to tie him down to a woman. The other two times, Bin-Kai had declined by saying he was still in school and not ready to settle. A traditional wife didn't appeal to him. He wanted someone with whom he could connect on an intellectual level.

What would be his excuse this time? He knew he should listen to his father. Raised up within traditional values, he adored his parents, obeyed them, and did his best to be their first and best son. He had followed his father's advice to attend Tsinghua University and had been grateful that his father had supported his five-year education there. After Mr. Zhou lost his business, the family income dropped to a regular worker's salary, causing financial difficulty. Even his mother, with her 3-inch feet, had had to find a job to earn money. She hadn't grown up that way and had never worked a day in her life. But even without these family sacrifices, Bin-Kai would still listen to his father because he was a wise man.

But his heart told him otherwise. He'd found the girl he had always dreamed of. With so few female students on Tsinghua University campus, he'd never had a girlfriend. Every girl he laid his eyes on already had an army of admirers and usually one victor. He was glad to see there were available female engineers when he joined the institute. But none of them had excited him. Then this angelic girl bumped into him in the bathhouse lobby. And she was available! Well, he'd heard rumors she had a boyfriend. But she never mentioned him. And she'd been receptive to his advances right from the start.

How could he convince his parents that Jun was the right girl for him?

They only spent two days with her. Maybe they'd change their mind if they got to know her better. I'm sure they would. They're reasonable people. I need to convince them Jun is the right wife for me.

He wanted to see Jun. But she'd rejected him in the canteen.

What did it mean? Was she still mad at me? She looked so ill, but she seemed polite. It wasn't just politeness, though; she seemed less excited to see me. What a bastard I was. I want a chance to prove I can be better. I want to prove we can be happy together.

25

CROSSROADS

It was October 1962. The fall weather in Hohhot fluctuated a lot, with warm days and chilly nights. Jun bundled up with a thick sweater and went for a walk after dinner. Recalling how warm it had been earlier that day, she decided she wouldn't need mittens or a hat.

The air was brisk. The poplar trees around the properties and on roadsides were becoming quite bare, their leaves in layers along the roadside. They hadn't had time to dry yet from the heavy rain in the afternoon.

Jun looked up. There was no moon. She could see the stars clearly and remembered what her mom had told her, about each star representing a life. She stood there, recalling the fallen stars in her life.

Where do fallen stars go? Do they stay up there still because people, like her, talked to their past loved ones while facing the sky? Do falling stars ever meet again?

As she walked further away from the compound, it became darker and chillier. She pulled her cardigan more tightly closed. She felt darker and chillier on the inside, too.

What to do, what to do?

She couldn't think of anyone from whom she could seek advice, let alone comfort. Tomorrow after work, she would lead a routine gathering of the Communist Youth League. As a leader, she was supposed to be a role model for others to follow. What a shame had befallen her—what would people say when they found out she was pregnant before getting married? And Bin-Kai.

I hate myself for being so stupid and not refusing him!

Jun slipped on a pile of leaves and landed on her bottom. She used her hands to support herself. Her hands and her pants were wet now. She struggled to get up. The slippery leaves wouldn't let her, and she kept falling back into the pile.

Jun got up from the ground but couldn't hold still and fell back to the ground again. She continued to get up and fall. Her face became muddy, and her hands bloody from constantly scraping against small rocks on the ground.

She wept, loud and long. All around her was deep darkness, with only a tint of light from far away. No one could hear her. She was all alone. Alone with the stars in the sky.

***

Another week had passed since the canteen encounter. Bin-Kai hadn't seen Jun. He'd tried to approach Mimi, but she ran as soon as he walked toward her. Then Bin-Kai got a call from the institute leadership.

Lao Wang was the communist party leader, one of the top two executives at the institute. Each organization had two top leaders—one was in charge of the intellectual and production aspects, with the other overseeing the political, mental, and social aspects.

This was only the second time Bin-Kai had met Lao Wang, the first being when he'd welcomed Bin-Kai to the institute on his first day.

"Hasn't it been over a year since you joined? How's work so far?" Lao Wang began.

"It's been good." Bin-Kai was uncertain what this was about. It must be serious, if Lao Wang was meeting with him in person.

"I've heard your project team leaders sing your praises. You're a star engineer and a project leader in the making. We're glad to have you here."

Bin-Kai suspected this must be what the meeting was about. He sat there quietly.

"Let's jump right to the point. Are you aware that Jun tried to kill herself?" Lao Wang held his teacup in both hands.

What?!

Bin-Kai jumped up from his chair, his jaw dropping in astonishment.

Lao Wang gestured for him to sit down.

"The nurse found her unconscious after her roommate reported it. She ate rat poison. We're lucky to have saved her." Lao Wang watched Bin-Kai's face closely. "The nurse has also informed me that Jun is pregnant."

Bin-Kai jumped up again. His eyes widened and his mouth formed an O. His face changed rapidly from disbelief to amazement and finally to guilt.

Lao Wang gestured to him to sit down again, and continued,

"This is a serious matter. We've had no suicides during my tenure here, and we don't want it to happen. I've talked with Jun. Eventually, she admitted you were the one who impregnated her." Lao Wang paused again and looked at Bin-Kai with keen eyes. As a seasoned leader, he knew how to speak in such a way that he could guide the listener in the direction of his choosing.

"Is it true? If so, we'll kick you out of the institute for good and report you to the police for rape. You'll go to jail."

Bin-Kai needed all his strength to stay seated. He took a moment to compose himself, then replied,

"Rape? It wasn't…"

"Well, it's your word against ours. Who do you think the authority would believe?"

"I didn't know she was pregnant. I made her mad a few weeks ago, and I didn't know what to do to mend it. She had been distant toward me. All this time, I thought she was just still mad at me. If I'd known she was pregnant, I would have…"

He didn't finish, just put his hands on his head and slumped forward. He knew he would have pushed aside his pride and fly to her side to comfort her and care for her.

"So, the baby is yours?" asked Lao Wang.

Bin-Kai straightened his upper body. "Yes, it must be. Well, we, umm… I believe so."

Lao Wang looked at him again with hawk eyes.

"Young man, you'd better watch your behavior. Now, what do you plan to do about the situation?"

"I don't know. I need time to think." Bin-Kai blurted out.

"You have no time to think. You have only one option if you want to keep your job, stay out of jail, and save a beautiful young woman's life—and the baby's, too."

Bin-Kai looked up at Lao Wang. He knew what Lao Wang meant.

"Yes, I'll marry her," he said firmly, then hesitated. "But does she want to marry me?"

"It's the right thing to marry her. It will be up to you to convince her. And do it as soon as possible. Let her know your heart, your decisions, and your intentions. If you both agree to marry, I'll talk to the housing department to secure a unit for you two. All you'll need to do is get the marriage license, which can be done in an afternoon. And you won't work on any remote projects for a while, not until after the baby comes."

***

Tump—Tump—Tump—Tump!

Jun was alone—Mimi was out—when she heard the familiar but now much faster steps on the stairs. Her heart pounded heavily, and blood rushed to her head and whole body. She had wished to see him despite her anger and pride. Now she realized that all she wanted in the whole world was to see him.

He knocked quickly, over and over.

Jun got out of bed and walked to the door.

He was still knocking when Jun opened the door.

Bin-Kai stepped in without a word. He pulled Jun into his arms and held her as tightly as if she might fly away otherwise. Jun let him. His heavy breath and the feel of his heartbeat comforted her. They stood there for a long time without speaking. Emotion totally consumed Jun, tears rolling down her face. She couldn't help but sob, her body shaking. Bin-Kai kept one arm tightly wrapped around her and used his other hand to wipe her tears away.

"Hush. It's okay. It'll be alright. Stupid me. I shouldn't have upset you. I didn't know you were pregnant. And I should have come and visited you. Here, come and sit." He led Jun to the edge of the bed, and she sat down. He walked to the washbowl and got a damp, clean towel. Gently, he wiped Jun's tears, examining her face as if it was a work of art. He leaned forward and kissed her eyes, forehead, nose, and lips.

Jun didn't speak, but her heart was racing, and she felt dizzy. She'd dreamed of Bin-Kai visiting her. Now he had—and she could see his sincerity and tenderness. When he kissed her, she felt consumed with passion, as if her blood was bursting out of her skin. She couldn't help but respond to his kiss hungrily. She realized how much she loved him and how much she needed him. All her anger and pride disappeared. She wanted to be with him, in his arms, under his chin (he loved to put his chin on top of her head), showered with his kisses.

Bin-Kai held her face with both hands and looked into her eyes. She looked back. Bin-Kai smiled. She hesitated a moment, then smiled back.

Bin-Kai said gently, "Let's get married. We'll have a family."

Jun put her hand on her stomach. Bin-Kai put his hand on hers. She looked at him, her big black eyes saying, "Can you say it one more time?"

Bin-Kai beamed. He kissed her lips and said, "Will you marry me?"

Jun paused another moment. Things were happening so fast. There wasn't much time to do any deep processing. She only had time to do a quick check: *Would I marry him even if I wasn't pregnant? I believe I would.*

She looked into Bin-Kai's eyes and said, "I would marry you even if I wasn't pregnant. So yes, I'll marry you."

***

There was an announcement of the marriage, but no official ceremony, which wasn't unusual. People struggled to fill their stomachs, and few had either spare money or high enough spirits for weddings. Several couples did similar things. They moved to the housing block for married couples, announced it, and that was that—they were married.

"Move a bit left. Too much. A little right. It's good now." Jun was directing Bin-Kai as he hung a frame of an enlarged photo on the wall of their new home.

Bin-Kai stepped down from a chair and walked toward the door where Jun was standing. He kissed Jun and stood by her, admiring the photo. It was the photo they'd used on their marriage license. "What a handsome couple," he said.

He looked at Jun and continued, "You could be more youthful looking in it, but it's not half bad, given your health these days."

She looked at the photo, too, then turned to look at him. "I agree—we make a super handsome couple, the best-looking couple in the entire institute."

Bin-Kai kissed her again and walked toward the desk on the other side of the room. He examined the same photo in a much smaller size and put it in the envelope that contained a letter to his parents.

"Ma and Ba, I'm writing to you with exciting news. I married Jun and we're expecting our child, your first grandchild. I know you'll support me because, as you said, it's time for me to settle down. And I know you have been expecting a grandchild for so long. We'll bring your grandchild to see you as soon as we can."

He opened the drawer, took out a box of photos—Jun merged their separate photo collections into the box—and put the negative and extra copies of their marriage photo into the box. Before putting the box back, Bin-Kai found an envelope sitting at the bottom of the drawer. Curious, he opened it and dumped its contents on the desk. There were about twenty-some photos dating back to when Jun was a young girl in middle school. Some photos had one person in it, some two, and some several people. One thing in common among all these photos was a young man, warm, handsome, relaxed, and smiling.

Bin-Kai's blood rushed to every part of his body. A twinge of jealousy shot through him.

Her first love!

He spilled the words out with an effort to keep them silent. He had an urge to tear these photos apart or else dump them in the trash can.

What's his name?

He realized he'd never heard Jun mention his name.

Right. She never mentioned him in front of me. Well, to be fair, she had the right to date anyone before she met me. Now, she's married to me. Me!

He thought for another moment. He had to do something, any-thing. Picking up one photo of Jun and the young man smiling at him innocently, he shut his eyes for a second. With shaking hands, he carefully tore the photo into two parts, separating the couple. He put the two pieces and the rest of the photos back in the envelope, put the envelope at the bottom, and put the box on top of the envelope.

She worried about everything, as far as giving birth and taking care of a baby were concerned. She remembered hearing about the tough experience Peifang had had when giving birth to Tiger—she'd lost a lot of blood. Xiaohe's story was worse. "It took so long for the baby to come out—the doctor had to cut me open to get him out. I almost died. Because I have such a small frame, people warned me a pregnancy could kill me."

C-sections were considered dangerous and even deadly.

Bin-Kai suggested, "Maybe we should go to my parents' home to have the baby. My mom gave birth to five children. She has experience and knows which midwives have an excellent reputation and what to do to recover afterward."

Jun hesitated. She recalled Lao-Si's rather indifferent glances and comments during her first visit.

Bin-Kai followed. "Don't worry. I'll go with you. You're family now. You're carrying their grandchild. They'll treat you well."

Jun thought about it. Where else could she go? Who else could she learn such things from? In the library, she couldn't find any books on the topic, even after going through all the bookshelves. She didn't want any colleagues to know about the pregnancy, so she didn't approach any of the mothers or older women to ask questions.

"I'll go."

After Jun submitted a request for a leave of absence, Lao Wang called her into his office and asked, "How far are you in your pregnancy?"

"About eight and a half months," replied Jun.

"Are things going well with Bin-Kai?"

"Yes. He's very kind and caring."

"Good. I've been meaning to talk with you. You've been a model engineer. I hear much praise from your team leaders. I'm glad to know your personal life and the pregnancy haven't interfered with your work. Since we cannot provide monetary compensation, I'd like to reward you with 40 vacation days."

Jun's eyes glistened. Lao Wang reminded her of her father.

"I'll work harder to make up the missed work when I return." Jun said determinedly, blinking back tears.

"I know you will. Have a safe trip."

27

LIANLIAN

The two younger brothers stood at the gate to greet Jun and Bin-Kai.

"Welcome back!" Shorty Bin-Nan said, grinning ear-to-ear.

"Ma said you brought a baby. Where's the baby?" Naughty Bin-Pei held a steamed bun, and his mouth was half full. He circled around Jun.

"You'll see," Bin-Kai patted Bin-Pei's back.

The room was warm and well-lit. Mr. Zhou and Lao-Si sat at their respective places at the kang table.

"Ma, Ba." Jun bowed slightly to them.

Mr. Zhou left his seat and said, "Come and sit here. It's warm on this side of the kang."

Lao-Si looked at Jun with warmth on her face.

Phew! Jun silently exhaled. She took off her coat, hat, scarf, and mittens. Bin-Nan brought in a cup of tea, and she held it with both hands. Its warmth extended to her arms and legs and reached her heart.

Lao-Si examined her. "It must be a small baby," she commented, then went back to sewing.

"What are you sewing?" Jun asked, making small talk.

"The baby's clothes. See?" Lao-Si displayed a small coverall without sleeves or leg parts.

"Ooh! I like it!" Jun exclaimed. She'd had little time to prepare baby clothes. She was about to jump off the kang to go look at it.

"Sit, sit! We'll have enough time to prepare all the baby stuff. I'll show you tomorrow what I've already made. Now, dinner is ready. The East Room is warm and ready for you two," Lao-Si said, leaving little room for negotiation. But Jun didn't mind. She was warm from the inside out.

***

"It's a girl!" the midwife called out.

Lao-Si wiped the blood and white birth coating from the crying baby and swaddled the little body with a blanket. She brought the baby to the kitchen to show everyone.

"Oh, so tiny!" they all exclaimed.

"Yeah, so little. She's smaller than her Ba's shoe," said Lao-Si. She turned to the baby, and a tender expression came to her face. "You came early, huh? Your Ba should be here any moment to see you."

The midwife said, "Better let her nurse the baby."

Lao-Si turned around and returned to the room.

The next day, Bin-Kai arrived. He had left Jun with his family and returned to work. Only two days later, he'd received a telegram telling him Jun had gone into labor much sooner than expected. He jumped on the next train even though he couldn't get a seat.

"They're doing fine," Mr. Zhou said when he entered the kitchen.

Rushing in, Bin-Kai threw open the East Room door.

Jun was in bed. A scarf wrapped around her head to prevent any potentially cold air. Next to her was a wrapped bundle.

"It's not a boy," said Jun. Bin-Kai had made several comments about playing with his son when they'd been talking about the pregnancy and the baby.

"She's so small!" He was surprised. He couldn't remember ever seeing a human this tiny.

"Yeah, only about 3 Jin." One Jin is 0.4 Kilogram or 1.1 Pound.

"It's not your fault. She came early, plus there wasn't enough food around when you were pregnant. Hopefully she'll catch up." Bin-Kai continued to examine the little face. "Can I hold her?"

Lao-Si came in. She picked up the baby and showed it to Bin-Kai.

"She's much smaller and weaker than your two brothers were at birth. Be careful. Use your hand to hold her head and upper body this way. Her neck is very fragile—don't assume she'd be able to hold herself up."

Bin-Kai grasped the baby, who was slightly longer than his hand. The baby cried. He looked at his mom. Lao-Si gestured to him, "Rock her like this." He did, and the baby's voice quieted. He couldn't take his eyes off her.

"Her face looks like an old man with lots of wrinkles. A cat would be bigger than her," he said, speaking without thinking to filter his words.

Jun cleared her throat pointedly. She felt an urge to defend the baby, but she couldn't find the words.

Lao-Si said blankly, "Don't you say anything like that! All babies are ugly at birth. They work hard to get out and have no energy left to make themselves look pretty. She looks fine to me! Plus, she has your eyes and chin. Look at the chin dimple! It's yours!"

Bin-Kai murmured, "Yes, Ma."

The next day, Mr. Zhou presented a piece of paper with the official name of the baby to Bin-Kai. He explained, "Since it's a girl, we can't use the family's generational name. Your Ma and I came up with this name. You can talk it over with Jun and then we'll apply for a Hu-Ko and the birth certificate for the baby. This way, Jun will get special supplies for being a new mom."

A Hu-Ko was a certificate of citizenship. The supplies included brown sugar, eggs, red dates, goji berries, ginger, and other various specialty foods. The government controlled all foods and goods and allocated them through ration coupons. It restricted these items from the public.

The month after childbirth was called The Month and the new mom was expected to be confined to the house. People believed that the first month after childbirth was crucial for the mother to recover from any physical trauma. If any of the problems or issues didn't resolve or if fresh problems occurred within the month, those problems would be liable to never go away, unless they were cured during The Month of a future birth.

There were other superstitions. The new mom shouldn't leave the room to avoid wind invading her body, she shouldn't do any physical labor including lifting anything, shouldn't drink cold water or eat cold food, shouldn't use cold water to bathe or wash any part of the body, and shouldn't expose her skin to avoid developing skin problems. She shouldn't cry or else she'd lose her eyesight. She should consume special foods to replenish the blood she'd lost and help her regain her strength. Popular meals included eggs, hot brown-sugar soup, or an old hen, boiled with some Chinese medicine and herbs such as Goji berries and red dates.

Someone had to care for the new mom, whether or not it was her first birth. So much so that being a nursemaid for new mothers was a whole career track. Some nursemaids built a reputation for doing a great job and new mothers' families would seek them out and reserve their services.

The new mother's room should only allow certain people to enter—mother-in-law, a nursemaid, the baby's father, and doctors, in case of emergency. The Month, as many mothers fondly called it, was the highest reward of being a mom. A new mother who couldn't have The Month was considered unfortunate and the object of pity. People would blame or judge her family for being inhumane or incapable.

Jun found all the attention and great food enjoyable and even thrilling, but she didn't realize there were superstitious underpinnings. Her sister-in-law Peifang had gone to her own parents' home to give birth to Tiger, so Jun had never witnessed all the entitlement and glory of The Month. She thought what she was receiving was simply because of the kindness of Bin-Kai's parents—it was their love for her.

Bin-Kai looked at the name from his parents: Zhou Baozhen. Both Bao and Zhen mean treasure, jewel, and precious things. The baby was doubly precious, in the eyes of his parents. He nodded and went to the East Room.

Zhou Baozhen 周宝珍

The name pleasantly surprised Jun. She had been uneasy that the baby wasn't a boy. The name, however, suggested Bin-Kai's parents still valued a baby girl.

More than valued, they considered her to be doubly precious.

Jun wouldn't have known if she hadn't seen the name. She looked at the characters for a long time and sounded the name out repeatedly.

Bin-Kai said, "Ba said if we want, we can come up with a nickname for the baby."

"Can we? That'd be great. This name sounds very official. A nickname would be good for us to use daily."

"I agree. Let's see, what should we call her?"

"Something unique. Baozhen could apply to any precious babies, and there could be many girls with the name Baozhen. It's meaningful to her grandparents. Maybe we could give her a name that's meaningful to us," said Jun.

"What did you have in mind?" Bin-Kai asked.

"I want her to be unique, daring, strong. I also want her to remind us, you and I, that we're building a family."

Bin-Kai nodded.

"How about we name her Lian, the Chinese Lotus?" She wrote the character on a piece of paper:

Lian 莲

"The lotus grows in mud and in unfavorable environments; it stands out in the water; its flowers, the water lilies, are beautiful and long-lasting." Jun paused a bit, took a breath, and continued,

"This lower part of the character means connection and linkage. The baby links you and me and makes us a family. She's also the one to link me to your parents. I hope she reminds us to stay connected."

"Good! I haven't seen many women with this name, so it'll be unique."

"Exactly." Jun was glad Bin-Kai took her suggestion.

"Aren't you cute, Lian?" Bin-Kai turned to the baby. He said again, "Aren't you pretty, Lian Lian?"

"Ah, it sounds better to use the double for a baby. We'll use Lianlian as her nickname," Jun exclaimed.

When The Month was over, Bin-Kai came again to escort Jun and Lianlian back to Hohhot.

Mr. Zhou said, "You're both going to be working full-time. If it's too much, we can help care for the baby."

Lao-Si added, "We raised our two younger sons without breast milk."

"You said a mom's breast milk is the best for a baby. She needs to catch up and my milk is abundant, so she'd better stay with me. I think we can handle it. We have many colleagues with young children," Jun justified.

"Sounds good. Let us know if you need help," Mr. Zhou said before they took off to the train station.

28

SHANSHAN

June of 1964 was pleasant in Hohhot. The air was dry and warm but not hot. The days were long and sunny. If there was rain, it'd be over quickly. June was one of the best months of the year.

"Mama! Mama!" Fourteen-month-old Lianlian reached out with her small arms to Jun as soon as Bin-Kai brought her home from the babysitter. He also brought dinner from the canteen.

"Hey, my baby girl. Sorry, Mama can't hold you anymore. You're getting heavy." Jun patted Lianlian's cheeks and gave her a bottle of milk. She put one hand on her lower back and sat slowly down on a chair by the kitchen table, which she'd already set for dinner. Lianlian held a water bottle and leaned her tiny body against Jun's thigh.

"This pregnancy differs from the first one. My back is killing me, and I'm tired all the time," Jun sighed.

"Good!" exclaimed Bin-Kai. Jun knew he meant this might be a boy. Given how much trouble she was having, and how big her belly was, she was hopeful, too.

That evening, her water broke. Bin-Kai sent Lianlian to the neighbors Xiaohe and Lao Kang and rushed Jun to the hospital.

The clock struck midnight, and the doctor claimed, "It's a big girl!"

Another girl! Jun's heart sank. At least this baby hadn't given her too much trouble during birth.

In the recovery unit of the hospital, Bin-Kai joined Jun. A nurse brought the baby for Jun to nurse. "A big healthy baby, 5 Jin and 9 Liang! (about 6 pounds)."

They both looked at the baby, then at each other, then back at the baby. The bundle was much longer and wider than Lianlian had been at birth, almost double the size. Her rosy face was round and full, with no wrinkles at all. Her eyes were wide open and had double eyelids, like Jun's. She was content. Her lips were instinctively sucking, the movement revealing two dimples, one on each side of the cheekbone.

"Dimples on her cheekbones," Bin-Kai murmured. He couldn't take his eyes off the baby as Jun moved her to one breast. The baby's eyes stayed open while eagerly nursing, her dimples deepening with each suck.

"Ooh! Take it easy, baby girl!" Jun exclaimed. She touched the baby's cheek and grinned at Bin-Kai. "She sucks hard! A lot stronger than Lianlian did."

"She's a pretty baby. I don't mind her being a girl at all," said Bin-Kai.

The next day, Bin-Kai took Lianlian to the hospital to visit.

Lianlian stood by the door and looked at Jun, a confused look on her face.

"Come to Mama, come." Jun sat in bed, one arm holding the baby to her chest. She gestured to Lianlian, but Lianlian didn't move. She stood there with her eyes on her mom. Her confusion shifted to something else.

"Darling Lianlian, don't be jealous. This is your Meimei (Chinese for younger sister)." Jun continued to beckon to Lianlian.

Lianlian gaped at Jun, then turned to Bin-Kai, who'd been watching the whole time. Bin-Kai grinned and picked her up. When both parents were present, Lianlian preferred Jun and wouldn't normally have voluntarily asked to be picked up by Bin-Kai. During the rest of the visit, Lianlian didn't look at her mom once. It took another day after her mom and the new baby came home for Lianlian to warm up to her mom again.

After some back-and-forth discussions, Bin-Kai and Jun settled on calling the baby Shan, or Shanshan, to match the double sound of Lianlian:

Shan 姗

To Jun, it was a perfect name for a girl. It meant being graceful. To Bin-Kai, the baby's calm demeanor and beautiful face reminded him of a girl in college he'd found attractive. Whenever this girl was walking in his direction, her long white skirt flew with the wind. Her steps were slow, steady, yet light, and altogether, she was elegant. Eventually, he learned her name was Shan and she already had a boyfriend. He didn't tell Jun about her, though. He wouldn't want to ruin Jun's fondness for the name.

Their two salaries combined still barely covered their living costs and the babysitter for Lianlian. In anticipation of additional expenses related to the new baby, they agreed not to hire a nursemaid for The Month. Jun regretted it immediately. She'd underestimated the workload involved with taking care of a newborn and a one-year-old while recovering from the birth. Shanshan hardly ever cried, but she ate a lot, almost non-stop, and peed and pooped a lot, using up clean cloth diapers quickly. Bin-Kai worked during the day and helped during lunchtime and after work. When he wasn't working, he spent his time washing and drying the cloth diapers, which were made from used cloth and bedsheets. Lianlian went to the babysitter's during the day and stayed home during the evenings and weekends. She needed to be fed, bathed, played with, and put to bed.

Jun couldn't get enough much-needed sleep. She found herself hungry and thirsty all the time. The food from the canteen wasn't satisfying. She had little time to cook the special food a new mother should have. Because she was feeling miserable, she became short-tempered. She couldn't help but cry from time to time. *Don't cry! They said you'll lose your eyesight if you cry during The Month.* She reminded herself, but she couldn't stop.

Bin-Kai was also overwhelmed. The institute was accommodating his situation of having a new baby by not sending him to a remote location. However, he was working on two projects and the workload was quite demanding. At home, he didn't know how to take care of a new mother for The Month. Whatever he'd heard from Jun or his mom about The Month hadn't really registered. He became more frustrated when Jun cried for no reason; she assumed he'd know something, but he didn't; and both babies needed his attention to feed and hold them, change their diapers, and rock them to sleep.

Jun and Bin-Kai argued during the first week of The Month.

"Don't you know I'm hungry? I'm feeding two people! And I'm so tired, so tired. All you do is wash the diapers," yelled Jun.

"It's not true. I'm doing most of the work! What did you do the whole day when I was at work and Lianlian at the babysitter's?" Bin-Kai countered.

"You don't know how exhausting it is to feed the baby non-stop! I have no time to sleep!"

"Of course I don't know. It's your job as a mother." Actually, he did know, because some nights he'd wake up when Jun had to feed Shanshan. But he didn't want to admit it, not right now.

Jun realized she had to find solutions herself. She couldn't go on like this anymore. Neighbor Xiaohe was out of the question because she'd told them ahead of time she was planning to visit her parents in Hunan Province, but Jun sensed she wasn't interested in helping at all.

Maybe I should ask Xia to come and help?

29

SHOCK

Xia was in her last year of college in Baotou, only a two-hour train ride away. She'd visited Jun a few months before, during the 1964 Spring Festival. On the first day, she noticed Bin-Kai ate most of the food without asking Jun or her. *I don't mind being neglected. But my sister is pregnant. Not only did he not ask her what she would like, but he ate like a pig as if no one else existed.*

On the second day, Bin-Kai brought home a few pieces of wood he'd found behind a building. Xia couldn't help but ask, "Are they free for you to take?"

The question surprised Bin-Kai. "No one was guarding them," he pointed out.

"That doesn't mean they're free. They look valuable and could be useful. Are you stealing?" Xia continued.

"What do you care?" Bin-Kai said and gave Xia an annoyed look.

On the third day, Xia saw Jun was the one who did laundry, even during her pregnancy. Xia used to do laundry when the two of them lived in the school. While Bin-Kai was out in the yard to work on those pieces of wood—he said he'd make a dining table out of them—Xia folded up her sleeves, grabbed a small stool, and sat down by the big washing bowl on the floor. She couldn't stand watching her sister bending over her tummy to wash the clothes.

As she splashed the water and merged the clothes into it, she murmured, "Yanshao would never have let you do laundry while you were pregnant."

Jun heard it and sighed. "It's all water under the bridge." She recalled countless nights she hadn't been able to fall asleep after her last visit to Yanshao. It had been a while since Jun last thought about him. Life had been too busy with work, Lianlian, and the second pregnancy.

"Is it? All forgotten? Do you know what happened to him? Do you care?"

Jun looked at her, alert. "Do you?"

"Yes. I visited him a month ago."

"What happened to him?"

"His mom died."

"I'm sorry to hear that..." Jun recalled the woman's calm face. *She wouldn't be too old and was in good health the last time I saw her. The last time would be what, two years ago? How time flies.*

"And they sent him to an institution."

"What? What kind of institution?" Jun felt like someone had slapped the back of her head.

"The kind for people who've lost their minds!" Xia let out the words with great effort.

People considered a mental institution to be worse than prison. Once someone had been sent to a mental institution, that person was marked as being wasted for life. It was a taboo deeply rooted in society.

Shock waves ran up and down repeatedly through Jun's body. She sat on the edge of the bed, unable to move, unable to speak. Her mind had gone blank. She couldn't see anything in front of her.

Xia's hands were busy rubbing the clothes, and she continued, "I didn't mean to bring this up. It's just... It's just so unfair! Every girl in our school admired him. Every girl! But he liked you, and only you. I came all the way here to go to college so I could visit you both. If I'd known you weren't going to marry him, if I'd known early enough..." She paused and used her sleeve to wipe her tears.

The room was quiet, dead quiet. Xia looked up. She saw Jun's eyes were wide open—she hardly blinked, her mouth was ajar, and her face was white-paper pale. She had a fixed stare.

Xia jumped up and walked toward her. Jun didn't seem to notice. Xia waved a hand in front of Jun but she stayed the same. Xia tapped Jun's shoulder. No response. Xia pushed her. Jun fell back into the bed, her eyes closed, and she was silent.

"Ahh!—Ahh!" Xia screamed hysterically.

Bin-Kai rushed into the room. He saw Xia standing by the bed, covering her mouth with her hands, her entire body shaking uncontrollably. He leaped forward, harshly pushing Xia away, and carefully lifted Jun from the bed. With his eyes on Jun's face the entire time, he held her in his arms, rocking her gently, and said quietly, "Jun, Jun. Can you hear me? Jun. Wake up."

Jun opened her eyes. It took a moment for her to realize where she was. Her gaze moved from Xia, to Bin-Kai, and back to Xia. Her eyes welled with tears and her sob became an anguished cry—a really loud cry.

It was a cry Bin-Kai had never heard from Jun. Neither had Xia, not even when their father died. Bin-Kai held her with one arm, wiping the tears from her face with the other, and he made a "Shh" sound in her ear as if soothing a crying baby. Xia ran around looking for a towel to bring to Jun. She also brought a cup of hot water. Then she stood by the wall and sobbed, too.

There was no telling how long this lasted.

At some point, Jun quieted down. She'd never felt so physically tired. Her head was heavy and foggy. She'd lost some sensation in her arms and legs. Her entire body felt like it was about to turn into a pile of dust. Her mind fixated on one single image—she was in the middle of a desert, alone and helpless.

With some effort, she glanced at Bin-Kai. With his help, she lay down in bed and closed her eyes. A short minute later, Bin-Kai and Xia heard slow, even breathing. Jun was asleep.

Bin-Kai put a cover over Jun. He walked into the hallway. Xia followed and closed the door behind her. Bin-Kai looked at Xia with an angry expression. "What did you do? What did you say to her?"

"I... we... I was telling..." Xia struggled to find words. Her whole body was trembling again. What had she done to her sister? Why did she have to tell Jun about Yanshao? And at this time in Jun's life and during her pregnancy? How selfish to let go of her anger that had built up. How stupid was she? What would she do if anything bad happened to Jun because of her big mouth and thoughtlessness?

Xia wiped her tears with a sleeve and said in a shaky voice, "I'm returning to school now."

Bin-Kai's facial expression changed little. "That's a good idea."

Xia quietly entered the room. After gathering her clothes and toothbrush, she stood by the bed and looked at Jun's sleeping face. She said in silence, "Sorry I disturbed you. I hope it didn't cause damage to the baby. You have the right to build a happy life. I hope you enjoy it. I promise I'll never mention Yanshao's name again. But I'll visit him as much as possible and do whatever I can to care for him."

Xia was relieved Yanshao still recognized her and was glad to see her whenever she visited. He'd even asked her for books, although the only books allowed were about Marxism, communism, and Chairman Mao's thoughts and poems—the so-called Red Books. She planned to bring more in future visits. She knew there might not be too many visits left because she was about to graduate from college and go with her fiancée, her college sweetheart, to wherever their placements ended up being.

30

SEEKING HELP

Jun shook her head.

No, Xia wouldn't be a good choice to help during The Month. She could only stay for a few days. She didn't know how to cook, let alone make those special meals new mothers should have. Also, she doesn't like Bin-Kai and might get into an argument with him again like last time when she visited. And, umm. There was something else last time. What was it?

Plus, what about after The Month? Bin-Kai wouldn't be home for most of the year. She'd have to take care of two young babies by herself. She barely managed to care for Lianlian during the last year without compromising work.

On the 9th day of The Month, after both babies went to sleep, Jun calmly spoke to Bin-Kai.

"I can't handle this anymore. We can't handle this. Even if we get through The Month, with you going away most of the time, what will happen to me and the two young babies?"

Bin-Kai had been contemplating the situation, too. Hiring help for The Month was an option, but it would cost money. Putting two babies at the babysitter's also cost extra money. Even with helpers or babysitters, it would still be such a struggle for Jun to be a single parent with a heavy workload.

"What ideas do you have?" asked Bin-Kai.

"I've been thinking about the offer your parents gave after Lianlian was born. We didn't need it then, but we need it now, even if only for a short period."

"Sending Lianlian to my parents?"

Having grandparents caring for the youngsters while parents working and earning money was a norm.

"Well. They love Lianlian. They named her 'double precious.' Remember the baby necklace your mom presented at Lianlian's 100-day celebration?"

People considered reaching 100 days old to be an important milestone for babies. At this age, babies were much stronger. They could hold up their heads and their backs, show an awareness of their surroundings, and interact with people consciously. This "birthday" celebration was a big event.

On Lianlian's 100-day celebration, Lao-Si brought out a cloth bag from a pocket close to her chest. Carefully untying it, she lifted the bag upside down and out slid a Qi-Lin necklace.

"This is a gift to my darling granddaughter. My three lady friends contributed, too. Now, Lianlian, let Nainai put this on your little neck."

Qi-Lin necklaces were jewelry made with light metals and gems, had complex designs, and were meant for precious babies from rich families. Having a Qi-Lin necklace was a big deal, signaling the baby's family was wealthy, and the baby was important to the family.

Bin-Kai went to the drawer and found the photo of Lianlian wearing the Qi-Lin necklace on her 100-day birthday. It was Lianlian's first photo ever.

He handed the photo to Jun. They stared at it together and turned their heads to look at the peacefully sleeping Lianlian.

How time had flown. Compared with the little baby in the photo, Lianlian looked so big and had such a mature face. Next to her, this new bundle was so immature, even though they were only fourteen months apart.

Bin-Kai gazed at Jun for a long while. With a slow and thoughtful tone, he said, "If we're going to ask them to help, we might want to give them the tougher task. Taking care of a newborn seems a lot harder."

Jun sighed. "But Shanshan needs my milk."

"I remember my mom didn't have milk for my two younger brothers. My dad would go to the gate to wait for the milk to be delivered. He would boil the milk to feed my brothers. My parents also fed the boys soup and rice porridge. The boys started eating regular food at a young age. I recall both my parents chewed the solid food themselves, then fed it to the boys. Look at how they look now. You wouldn't know the difference."

Jun remembered hearing that too from Lao-Si. She looked at each girl back and forth. Her heart was torn. She didn't want to be separated from either of them.

Bin-Kai said, "It's late. Let's go to bed now and think more tomorrow."

The next day flew by quickly. In the evening, while Jun was feeding Shanshan and Bin-Kai was washing the diapers, Lianlian fell by the stove. A cut on her left eyebrow bled, making her face look horrible.

It was a sleepless night for Jun and Bin-Kai.

The next morning, Bin-Kai made an executive decision. "I'll ask the babysitter to help you for the rest of The Month. We'll pay her extra to watch Lianlian here and help with chores. I'm taking Shanshan to my parents—I'll catch tonight's train."

Jun didn't argue. She was too exhausted to argue.

In the evening, Jun's breasts were full and unbearably painful. Shanshan had brought on more milk than Lianlian had. As Lianlian leaned over, her eyes pleading for food, a small patch on her cut, an idea came to Jun.

She held Lianlian to her chest and put one nipple into Lianlian's mouth. Lianlian sucked forcefully.

"You poor thing. I got very little nutrition while I was pregnant with you, and you got very little milk when I was pregnant with Shanshan. Now, drink, so you get stronger."

With the sucking sensation, Jun recalled Shanshan's cute face, how those two dimples would jump up and down with her sucking. Jun missed Shanshan terribly already. Her tears rolled down onto her clothes and on Lianlian's face. She wiped her tears and looked at Lianlian, who was looking up at her curiously with the nipple in her mouth. Jun gently smiled back at Lianlian. Releasing the nipple, Lianlian beamed at her mom brightly. "Mama! Mama!" Lianlian called out and touched Jun's chin with her tiny hand.

"My precious, I know you've had little attention lately. I was busy with your Meimei. Now, it's only you and me. You and me."

"Meimei. Where's Meimei?" Lianlian looked around. At fourteen months old, she spoke clearly and fluently.

"Meimei is with your Yeye and Nainai. We'll visit them soon, very soon."

***

Mr. Zhou and Lao-Si had expected to hear news about the birth of the second baby. The announcement letter never came.

Then, out of the blue, Bin-Kai entered the house with a bundle in his arms.

"Ma, she must be starving." Bin-Kai handed the bundle to Lao-Si.

"Ooh, what a pretty face!" Lao-Si exclaimed and went to feed Shanshan.

Mr. Zhou said, "No announcement. No discussion. You just bring the baby here?"

"Sorry Ba. We're struggling. Jun is not doing well. She's exhausted and cries a lot. Lianlian had an accident with blood on her face. We need help now. I have to catch tonight's train to get back."

Mr. Zhou nodded. "Of course, we'll help. You go back and do your best to take care of Jun and Lianlian."

31

YOUNG FIGHTER

It was early spring 1965. Coldness still dominated the air. It also occupied the hearts of Jun and Bin-Kai. They were on the train to Jinzhou, with Lianlian in their arms. They were about to say goodbye to Shanshan, who would be nine months old in two days. Mr. Zhou had been writing letters over the last six months to keep them informed about Shanshan's condition. The letter from yesterday was short and to the point:

> "The doctors don't think she can make it. We've hired a carpenter to prepare an infant coffin."

Shanshan's life with her grandparents did not begin smoothly. Six months ago, before turning three months old, Shanshan developed fevers and couldn't keep any food down. Mr. Zhou and Lao-Si took her to a nearby hospital. The doctors concluded she had meningitis. Mr. Zhou wanted to have a second opinion. They took Shanshan to Jinzhou Second Hospital, one of the best in town.

"Mr. Zhou?" A young doctor stopped in front of them in the lobby.

"Yes. And you are...?"

"I'm Li Mingde. My Ba Li Dashan used to work with you in the factory. He did accounting for you. You treated him very well."

Mr. Zhou remembered. "How is he doing these days?"

"He's doing well. Thank you for asking. Who is this cute baby?" Dr. Li turned his head to the red-faced bundle in Lao-Si's arms.

"My granddaughter Shanshan," answered Mr. Zhou.

Dr. Li put his hand on Shanshan's forehead. "High fever. Let me see what we can do." He called a nurse to take Shanshan inside and led Mr. Zhou and Lao-Si to his office. "Wait here. I'll be back."

A long while later, Dr. Li returned.

"We got some test results now and more results will come in a few days for confirmation. But from what I can tell, it doesn't look good."

"What is it? How bad?" Mr. Zhou asked.

"It's likely to be meningitis—a disease that's common these days, and afflicts mostly young babies."

Mr. Zhou made a mental note—the same diagnosis. He asked, "Is it curable?"

"We don't have enough evidence. So far, the survival rate is very low."

"If it's possible to survive, given what you said, can you try to save her?"

"Let me check a few things. I'll be back." Dr. Li left the room.

Mr. Zhou paced back and forth in the office.

Lao-Si sat in Dr. Li's chair and murmured with eyes closed, "How could this happen? How could this happen? Lao-Tian-Ye, you took our daughter away, then gave Shanshan to us as a replacement. Please don't punish us. I'll do anything you ask of me. Please don't let her die. Please save her."

Mr. Zhou paused, looked at her, and continued pacing. He was pondering the same thing.

How could Lao-Tian-Ye give Shanshan to us and take her away again? Our daughter died when she was three months old. Did she have the same disease? No one could diagnose her. Now, Shanshan became ill at the same age. Are we cursed? Why are we not able to keep a baby girl healthy past the three-month threshold?

Dr. Li came in. "Sit, sit. You must be tired." He gestured at Lao-Si, who had tried to stand up. He turned to Mr. Zhou.

"All the hospital beds are in use. But I secured one for Shanshan. We'll take her in and treat her. But it will cost some money. Here's a rough estimate for the bed and treatment. The actual cost may end up being different."

Mr. Zhou looked at the number. He and his wife couldn't afford it. But he had no other choice and no time to consult with his son. He nodded and said in a shaky voice,

"I'm sure my son and his wife will come up with the money. My other two sons can help too. Please reserve the bed and treat her. We cannot thank you enough."

"Don't thank me yet. We still don't know if she'll survive, but we'll try our best."

The treatment had lasted for the last six months. Mr. Zhou had received the dire news a few days ago.

Jun and Bin-Kai rushed to the hospital from the train station. They saw Mr. Zhou and Lao-Si sitting outside Shanshan's room.

"Shh... She's sleeping." Lao-Si raised her finger. She took Lian-lian's hand and pulled the girl into her arms. "Come to Nainai. You're growing fast."

"Come over here." Mr. Zhou led Jun and Bin-Kai to an area close to a nursing station. He didn't want Lao-Si to hear certain things.

"Dr. Li is going to try a drug named Penicillin on her. I had to sign a permission form. This drug just became affordable and is supposed to be powerful."

A nurse behind the counter heard them and said to Jun and Bin-Kai, "Shanshan is so lovely. Her smile is contagious."

Another nurse piped up, "Such a cheerful personality. She hardly ever cries and could spend hours playing with anything as a toy."

Bin-Kai nodded at them, and Jun wiped her tears and said, "Thank you!"

***

Dr. Li walked toward them and offered his greetings, followed by some news. "There are some signs of improvement, but it's too early to say whether she's out of danger yet. I suggest you all go home and rest now."

Bin-Kai drew Dr. Li aside. "Tell me the truth, Doctor," he said quietly. "How bad is this disease?"

"We're doing our best, but out of the four children with the same disease in this hospital, two have died," Dr. Li explained. "The third showed some limited improvement but may suffer permanent damage," Dr. Li said.

Bin-Kai asked anxiously, "What might happen to Shanshan? Could there be any lasting damage?"

"So far, we don't see any signs. The drug seems to work well on her. We can only hope. She's a fighter," said Dr. Li.

Jun and Bin-Kai returned to Hohhot with Lianlian. They left with some relief—the drug had apparently worked, and Shanshan was making steady progress.

32

SISTERS

One month later, Jun, Bin-Kai, and Lianlian visited Jinzhou again. Shanshan sat on the kang, with her legs curled and her tiny feet touching each other. Jun reached for her. Shanshan hesitated, then crawled over to Lao-Si, whereupon she turned and gave Jun an intense look.

Jun cried out, then began sobbing, and couldn't stop.

Shanshan survived! She's fine now. But she doesn't recognize me as her mom, and she prefers Lao-Si.

Lao-Si picked up Shanshan and said to Jun, "She's a strong girl. A dragon born at midnight. No one should dare challenge her."

Bin-Kai exhaled softly, watching Shanshan, whose hair was growing out in a thin layer—the nurses had shaved her hair to place the medical device trackers on her. Her eyes were enormous, out of proportion to her tiny and slim face. Her bony hands and arms had many black and purple spots, evidence of how many injections she'd had.

Shanshan turned her head and caught Bin-Kai's eye. She smiled with those two big dimples on her cheekbones and opened her arms to him. Bin-Kai's heart was overflowing with joy. He gathered her up and held her tightly in his arms.

A few moments later, Shanshan turned to look at Jun. She examined Jun's face carefully. Those dimples again appeared. She twisted, reaching out her arms to Jun.

Jun's tears wouldn't stop. She took Shanshan from Bin-Kai and kissed her cheeks and forehead over and over. She had never kissed a baby—or anyone, for that matter—in front of others.

"Here, this is your big jie jie. She's two years old." Jun squatted next to Lianlian, who was holding Jun's pants with one hand and a bottle with the other. Lianlian had been watching quietly.

The two girls sized each other up in silence. Shanshan reached out to touch Lianlian's cheek. Lianlian presented her bottle to Shanshan. They both laughed. Shanshan got so excited she flapped her arms like a bird. Lianlian stepped forward and embraced Shanshan.

In the evening, Shanshan gestured and made baby sounds, frustrated. She didn't stop until the grownups figured out she wanted Lianlian to sleep next to her. For the next two days, the two girls were inseparable. They sought each other from the moment they woke up. They each wanted to drink or eat whatever the other was drinking or eating and helped each other with eating and drinking. Lianlian crawled on the big kang to mimic Shanshan's crawling. Shanshan passed pieces of mud to Lianlian to eat—she had been crawling around and picking up pieces of mud around window corners and putting them in her mouth when no one was watching. They laughed and played as if nothing existed but the two of them. They became anxious if they couldn't see each other. "Mama, where's Shanshan?" Lianlian would ask anxiously. If Shanshan didn't see Lianlian, she'd look in all directions, then sob, despair on her face. Everyone would hurry to reunite the two of them.

Jun spent a lot of time watching both of them. Lianlian seemed so happy around Shanshan. She didn't grab Jun's hands or pants all the time anymore. She must have been lonely as an only child. Now, her mouth constantly curved into a smile. Her cheeks seemed filled with color during these two days. Jun had never heard Lianlian laughing so hard and so often. And Shanshan, Jun observed, was just as happy. She showed no sign of having spent most of her life so far fighting a life-threatening disease. Imitating Lianlian, including with speech, she had already learned a few words at just ten months old. If they were together all the time, Shanshan would develop much faster, and the two of them would play together and need minimal attention from a babysitter.

Together? Did I just imagine that?

The realization shocked Jun. There was no way she could take both girls back to care for them. Even with a babysitter during the day, Jun was exhausted taking care of Lianlian at night and over the weekend. With two babies, Jun still had to care for them for all the tedious tasks. Plus, Shanshan would soon learn to walk. It was a dangerous stage, and injuries could easily happen. The scar on the corner of Lianlian's eyebrow from when she fell days after Shanshan's birth seemed to be permanent. Jun shivered when she thought of the possibility of the girls getting injured or sick again.

Mr. Zhou was observing, too. It was great to have Shanshan home finally instead of visiting her at the hospital daily. It was even more exciting to see her so happy around Lianlian. He had ordered one bottle of milk per day since Shanshan was home. When Lianlian arrived, he told the milk delivery man to add one more bottle. "My other granddaughter is home, too," he explained joyfully. "For a brief visit or a long stay?" the milk deliverer asked. "Let's just keep the milk coming until I tell you to stop."

Somehow, he had a hunch Lianlian would stay. He'd welcome that. Taking care of two babies wasn't harder than one. It'd be easier. It would be a dream come true. The house would finally have babies in it, laughing and playing. Their laughs and even cries would be music to his ears. He knew his wife would agree with him. She was the one doing the daily chores. But she was so light on her feet and had no complaints at all. She had suffered a great deal during the past few months. It would be hard to imagine if Shanshan ever left her. Mr. Zhou could see Lao-Si would wholeheartedly welcome Lianlian to stay. Hadn't it been her wish when Jun finished The Month after giving birth to Lianlian? Shanshan was a godsend to Lao-Si. It would make her so happy if she could have both granddaughters with her.

It was dinnertime on the day before Jun and Bin-Kai were to return to Hohhot. Sitting on Lao-Si's lap, Shanshan kept her eyes on Lianlian the whole time, subconsciously opening her mouth when a spoon arrived at her lips, then swallowing without chewing. She was a good baby who'd eat anything. Lianlian, facing Shanshan while sitting on Jun's lap, looked up and beamed at Shanshan with each bite of her own dinner, which she ate without help. The air was tense among the grownups, though. They were silent, even the two uncles.

Mr. Zhou cleared his throat and, breaking his own house rule of not talking while eating, asked, "Have you two thought about what to do with the girls?"

Bin-Kai looked at his parents and Jun, contemplating. "We want to know if we could leave Lianlian here as well. It would help us a great deal."

Jun agreed, adding, "You're great caregivers, and I trust you. I'll miss Lianlian. Well, I'll miss both girls terribly. But I'll visit as much as possible."

Mr. Zhou didn't speak. Lao-Si stopped feeding Shanshan and looked on.

Bin-Kai continued, "We know this can be costly. We can provide more money to buy milk and food for the girls."

Mr. Zhou put down the chopsticks. "Nonsense. They're our blood and we don't need your money. We covered Shanshan for the past ten months and we can cover Lianlian as well. Plus, train tickets will cost you quite a bit."

Bin-Kai and Jun stared at Mr. Zhou with excitement. Bin-Kai burst out, "You mean you'll take Lianlian in?"

Mr. Zhou nodded, affirming this would be the best solution for all involved.

"Yeah!! Yeah!!" Naughty Bin-Pei jumped to his feet. He loved playing peek-a-boo with Shanshan, making her giggle uproariously.

"Well, we didn't expect this before this trip. We don't have all of Lianlian's clothes with us," Jun hesitated.

"How much clothing does she have? We can manage. Bring them next time you visit. Shanshan might use some of them," Lao-Si said and went back to feed Shanshan, who was holding Lianlian's hand. Lianlian was leaning toward Shanshan with her spoon—it almost touched Shanshan's lips and the food fell off the spoon onto the floor. They all laughed.

33

PROMISE

Jun worked overtime on evenings and weekends so she could save three working days each month to visit the girls. She volunteered to be assigned short-term remote projects to earn extra vacation days and remote work compensation, and even though it wasn't much, every bit helped. She and Bin-Kai were still in debt to friends and relatives who'd loaned them money for Shanshan's treatment. They had insisted on compensating Bin-Kai's parents for the ongoing cost of milk for the girls, which was luxury food and relatively expensive. Train tickets also ate up their double salary income.

It was time for annual performance evaluations and salary raises. Project team leaders evaluated their members, and management synthesized the results.

Lao Shao, the head of Jun's division, called her to his office.

"I've reviewed your record. You've made steady improvements over the years. This year, you earned a score of 5 out of 5 in all seven areas, the highest since you joined the institute, and the highest among your peers. Your team leaders speak highly of you, not only in the intellectual aspect but also in work ethics, team collaboration, and a positive attitude toward work. Several of the leaders mentioned you could hold your own and take care of a significant part of a project. You're one of our few star engineers. Your political position has been very good, too. Although not heading the youth league anymore, you've been attending all the political meetings enthusiastically. You haven't done or said anything to raise eyebrows. If you continue to stand on the Red side, support the party enthusiastically, and be a star performer, we might invite you to join the communist party as a member."

Lao Shao's words pleased and assured Jun. She knew she wouldn't face being warned about under-performance. Two of her colleagues had received the warning last year, and their reputations had been destroyed. Few teams wanted to take them in, and their prospects of promotion faded. Jun knew her leaders were happy with her performance because she could deliver high-quality work at a faster pace than others—with fewer errors or redoes. Also, unlike her colleagues, she didn't ask for help. If there was something she didn't know, she would simply figure it out.

The most exciting part of Lao Shao's comments was about joining the communist party. She had worried her family class of "Rich People" would prevent her from being considered. Candidates for the communist party were usually from the "Worker" and "Peasant" classes.

Now, Lao Shao seemed to imply her family class might not be an issue to join the party, and that it was up to her behavior.

"I thank the leaders for evaluating me with such high marks." Jun felt a bit tongue-tied.

"We recognize quality work, and we appreciate quality work. We're also always on the lookout for star performers as potential leaders." By this, he was implying there were opportunities for promotion.

Jun was excited to hear that. Maybe she would finally be promoted. She had noticed in the past promotions happened to those who were communist party members and who were highly competent at their jobs.

Earning 5 out of 5 in all areas gave her the confidence she could do her job at the highest level. Once she became a communist party member, she would be on her way to being promoted to higher positions.

"For the salary, we're fortunate to be able to offer a raise," Lao Shao continued. "You'll get 3% more next year."

That was great news, especially considering her salary hadn't changed for the past few years.

"Is the salary raise related to job performance?" asked Jun, wanting to know for certain rather than speculate.

"No. As usual, the rate depends on the education level of the employee. This year, college graduates get 5%; vocational school graduates get 3%."

Jun didn't speak.

Lao Shao explained, "This rate is set by the government as part of the salary structure. We cannot override it because all institutes follow the same pay scale. The only thing we can do is to recognize and praise high achievers like you, offering a pride that's more important than money. Don't you agree?"

"Yes," said Jun. She could see why each institute wouldn't be able to do much about the salary but could decide how it operated, and the promotion criteria could be local to the institute.

"Do you have questions or requests?" asked Lao Shao.

Requests would be like borrowing money or generating negative credits. She already had a request in place and didn't dare to have more.

"No. Only the current arrangement of three days per month saved to see my daughters in Jinzhou."

"Very well. Congratulations on a productive year." Lao Shao gestured to the door and lowered his head to check a pile of papers on his desk.

Jun returned to her desk. Her mind couldn't stop running over and over the "3% vs. 5%." When she had graduated, she'd been thrilled to join the institute. She would have taken the job at any salary. When she found out her colleagues with college degrees earned a lot more than she did, she was uneasy. But she had told herself that the cost and time of receiving a college degree justified the difference. Still, when she picked up monthly salaries for Bin-Kai and herself—when Bin-Kai was out of town—she'd begun to feel bitter. Over the past couple of years, the bitterness had calmed down a bit because there'd been no change in any salaries. Now, there'd finally been a raise, and the difference in salary had only gotten larger.

If having a college degree was an actual indicator of capability and job performance, it might help justify the 2% difference between the raises. But it wasn't at all. Jun had noticed many of her co-workers with a college degree were unable to resolve issues or improve processes. Most of them had an average job performance.

If I could relive my life, I'd go to college no matter what, Jun said to herself. This was not the first time she'd said this.

34

RED GUARDS

Carrying two bags of food she had gathered over the past two months, Jun stepped out of the train station and walked toward her in-laws' home. Lianlian had now turned three and Shanshan had turned two. Although one year apart, the girls looked like twins. They were about the same size, had the same hairstyles, and dressed in the same clothes—it was easy to make two garments out of the same fabric. Whenever they were out of the house, they'd draw a lot of attention from people, since twins were rare, and people had a fun time guessing who was who. They had also earned much praise from the neighbors for being adorable and well-behaved.

It was 1966. The country was in the early stage of the Cultural Revolution. This socio-political movement was bent on preserving communism by purging all remnants of capitalist and traditional elements from the Chinese society. The movement would go on to last ten years.

Like Hohhot, the streets in Jinzhou had the feel of people on alert. Even on this sunny and warm day, few people lingered or chatted with each other. People seemed to be cautious.

Jun was almost at her in-laws' house. Suddenly, she heard loud footsteps and a large group of people yelling,

"Stay away! Clear the road!"

She quickly stood aside alongside everyone else and watched, curious. Then, with horror, she watched a group of ten young Red Guards storm into Mr. Zhou's yard. They wore green uniforms with a red armband on their left arm. Some of them carried long guns. Most of them looked like teenagers.

"What's going on?"

"Let's see."

Passers-by whispered to each other and followed the Red Guard to the yard. Jun rushed along with them.

Several Red Guards stood by the house door, which was wide open. Two Red Guards dragged Mr. Zhou out of the door and pushed him to the center of the yard. Mr. Zhou's head was bowed, his gaze fixed on the ground. One Red Guard kicked his behind and yelled, "Stand still!"

Two female Red Guards pushed Lao-Si out of the door. They walked too fast, and she fell to the ground. "Get up! You dirty wife of a capitalist!" one of them shouted. The other woman followed. "Your small feet are firm evidence you represent the old ways and the rich!" Lao-Si sat on the ground, looking up at them. The two women bent down and lifted Lao-Si up, depositing her next to Mr. Zhou.

The sound of babies crying loudly floated out of the open door. Jun's heart froze—those were her babies! "Nainai!" "Yeye!" Bin-Nan and Bin-Pei rushed out of the door, each carrying a baby. Lianlian struggled to get free from Bin-Nan's hold. Bin-Nan put her down and Lianlian ran to Mr. Zhou and clung to his pants. He bent and picked her up. Shanshan kept calling "Nainai! Nainai!" Her arms reached for her grandmother. Lao-Si turned her head, her face filled with warmth at the sound. Bin-Pei let Shanshan run to Lao-Si.

Jun wanted desperately to rush over to her girls.

But wait! What can I do? There are ten of them. Think! Control yourself!

"Make the babies stop crying!" a Red Guard shouted.

Both Mr. Zhou and Lao-Si held the babies closely, their mouths made "Shh-shh" sounds to the babies. The girls hid their faces in their grandparents' bosoms and stopped crying.

The yard became crowded.

A Red Guard kicked Lao-Si's leg. "Lower your head!"

Lao-Si turned to look at him.

"Did you hear me? Lower your head!"

He pushed her head lower and put a dunce cap on her head that had black inked characters printed on it:

"Knock down the Capitalist!"

Another Red Guard put another dunce cap on Mr. Zhou.

A tall Red Guard who seemed to be the leader stood in the center. He looked around the crowd and said in a loud voice,

"Comrades! We're here today to let these two know we won't forget what they did in the past to get rich by taking advantage of the poor."

There were murmurs in the crowd. Jun recognized some as neighbors. Many were strangers.

The leader turned to the elderly couple. "Have you thought about the evil acts you did when you were a capitalist? Speak!"

Mr. Zhou didn't answer.

Lao-Si looked up. The hat almost fell off. She said in a steady voice, "My husband provided employment opportunities for the poor so they could earn money to support their families."

"Earn money. Listen to her! Poor people had to work hard to earn money!" The leader looked around the crowd again and back to Lao-Si.

"It's exactly what's wrong with the old system. It's exactly why our government had to take over the privately owned enterprises, so that the people—people like my family and like many other families—can have an enjoyable life without being forced into labor." He turned to the crowd again, raised his fist into the air, and shouted, "Knock down the capitalists!"

Some in the crowd, especially the young kids, repeated after the leader.

"Never let them come back!" he shouted again, and more people joined him.

With each chant of the slogan, the two babies buried their heads further into their grandparents' chests.

Jun watched with disbelief. Every shout and cry tugged at her aching heart. What a frightening moment this must be for the girls. She needed to get them out of here. She walked toward Bin-Nan, who was standing nervously by the side, shifting his weight from leg to leg. He gave Jun a look of recognition but said nothing.

Jun stood by Bin-Nan's side and whispered without looking at him, "Should we take the girls from them?"

"Don't believe we can. The babies will cry harder. That may draw more unwanted attention, and they may hurt the babies." Bin-Nan said, not looking at Jun, either. "Plus, with the babies in their arms, the Red Guard may have sympathy and go easy on them."

Using the babies as a shield?

Jun couldn't believe what she'd heard. But at that moment, there seemed nothing she could do to save the babies or her in-laws.

This entire time, Mr. Zhou had kept his head low and stared at the ground. Lao-Si never lowered her head. She wore an expression that said "We did nothing wrong. You're a bunch of dumb kids."

The Red Guard leader looked at Lao-Si.

"You don't seem to realize the evil things your husband did. We'll visit you more often to make you learn."

Bin-Nan murmured to himself, "Ma. Stop it. No use."

One of the Red Guards yelled, "That's right! We'll come back!" He threw an old ceramic jar—which he'd picked up from the shed—to the ground by the old couple. Another Red Guard used the butt of his gun to break it into pieces.

Shanshan screamed and started crying again. Mr. Zhou gave Lao-Si a glare. She lowered her head and whispered into Shanshan's ears. Shanshan stopped crying and pushed her head hard into Lao-Si's chest.

The leader waved his hand and said, "Let's go, Comrades. We're done with these two today. But we'll be back!"

The Red Guards left. The bystanders gradually left too.

Bin-Nan and Jun rushed forward, and each took a girl from the old couple. As soon as Shanshan left her arms, Lao-Si collapsed to the ground. The humiliation, the long period standing on her feet, and her fear for the babies were too much for her.

35

ESCAPE

That evening, Jun learned this was the second time the Red Guards had visited. It wasn't hard for the Red Guards to find out who was at the bottom of the classification list. Each citizen's demographic data was registered in Hu-Ko, and his or her major job changes and life events were recorded in Dang-An. Both were at the local government's office. Being classified as a capitalist, the worst among all classes (and on par with landlords), Mr. Zhou would be the first to be targeted by the Red Guards at the onset of the Cultural Revolution.

Mr. Zhou sat by the kang table, a teacup in hand. "We've seen similar things like this before. The best way to deal with this is to be obedient, to say less and nod more, and not to cause any confrontations at all."

"What a group of dumb kids, no older or more educated than Bin-Pei," Lao-Si said. She had trouble accepting the Red Guards' unfair treatment of her husband. His business had provided jobs for so many people. He'd been kind to all his employees. Before he donated his business to the government during the Joint State-Private Ownership movement in the early 1950s, he'd voided all the debts from many people. His company, or the one it merged into, still held the position of being the largest flour processing factory in the region. These things had made her proud, with a sense of superiority. Plus, hadn't her husband already been re-educated and cleared of all wrongdoing? He must have been, because the jail—well, the camp—let him out in eight months, sooner than the originally designated period. These Red Guards were about the age of her youngest son Bin-Pei, young and dumb. They weren't interested in hearing her explain about the past. All they cared about was Mr. Zhou being a capitalist. They shouted and pushed, used their bodies instead of their heads, and behaved as badly as if they were military troops in the war. They treated people with no respect at all. Someone had to tell them, to remind them they should treat people, especially older and good people, with decency, respect and even admiration.

Two days later, the Red Guards made their third visit. Once again, with their heavy footsteps and chanting their slogans, they marched into the yard.

Jun grabbed Lianlian into her arms and reached for Shanshan, but the baby ran into Lao-Si's arms. Within a minute, Mr. Zhou and Lao-Si were pushed into the center of the yard. The Red Guards did similar things with the dunce hats, chanted slogans, and destroyed more belongings.

Holding Lianlian tightly, Jun watched from the windows. Seeing Shanshan crying and clinging to Lao-Si made her furious. None of her in-law family members took Shanshan away.

Jun paced back and forth in the room. She needed to do something. But what could she do? Thoughts flooded her mind.

By now, people in the neighborhood or even from the institute would have known my in-laws are capitalists, or "black" people. Will people treat me as a capitalist too because I'm married to the family? It would ruin any chance I might have of joining the communist party, or of earning a promotion at work. Not only that, but would people regard the girls to be in the capitalist class, too?

Jun sat on the edge of the kang but got up only a few seconds later. She couldn't calm her body or mind.

There are so many uncertainties. But first thing first, the girls aren't safe here with the Red Guards visiting so often. They need to get out of here. But I don't believe my in-laws would agree. It seemed the girls provided some comfort to them. But the babies are frightened! I need to protect them from these traumatic and violent visits. We three must leave as soon as possible. Yes—we must leave immediately. But how? There's no way the in-laws would allow it. It'd be me against the four of them. Think. Think! How??

***

The next day, one day before Jun's planned departure day, she went out alone, returning later with five armed Red Guards.

Lao-Si was rocking Shanshan, who was asleep with a milk bottle nipple in her mouth. Lianlian was playing with Bin-Pei on the inner side of the kang. Mr. Zhou was sitting by the kang table, sipping tea. Bin-Nan was reading the newspapers.

One Red Guard stood outside the door. The other four entered the room. The leader who had been here during those last two visits said, "Pack for the babies. They need to leave with their mother immediately. Don't anyone try to do anything stupid."

That shocked everyone in the house. They looked at the Red Guards and at Jun.

"What?" Mr. Zhou asked.

"These two baby girls should not stay here. Their mother is taking them back to where they belong. They need to go right now," said the leader.

Jun didn't look at anyone. She was busy packing baby clothes and food into the bags she'd brought. She handed the bags to one Red Guard and walked to the kang table. "Lianlian, come to Mama."

Lianlian crawled over into her arms. Jun passed Lianlian to a female Red Guard and walked to Lao-Si. "Ma, I need to take Shanshan now. It's best for the girls to stay away for a while."

Lao-Si stared at Jun with fire in her eyes. "Don't you dare take her away from me!"

"Hey, old woman, give the baby to her Ma!" The Red Guard leader commanded.

Lao-Si turned her upper body and shielded Shanshan from anyone's reach. Bin-Nan moved closer to his mom. A male Red Guard moved closer to him.

Jun stood there, tears rolling down. "Ma, very sorry. But this is the best option for the girls."

"Over my dead body!" Lao-Si cried out. Shanshan woke up and cried. Her bottle fell to the kang.

"Don't make us use force." The leader said.

Mr. Zhou had been watching the entire time without speaking. He got off the kang, walked over to Lao-Si, and took Shanshan from her arms. He rocked Shanshan and said in a soft voice, "Hao bao bao (good baby). You're always our hao bao bao."

Shanshan stopped crying, looking at him, Jun, and Lao-Si. She reached for Lao-Si. But Mr. Zhou gave her to Jun, and said in a firm tone, "You're her Ma. We trust you'll treat her well."

Lao-Si got off the kang, intending to snatch Shanshan back, but she didn't land on her feet. She fell to the floor. Bin-Nan and Mr. Zhou went to pick her up.

"I will," Jun said in a quiet voice and walked out with Shanshan in her arms. The Red Guards followed. Both babies looked back and screamed.

"No—!" Lao-Si's heartbreaking scream stayed with Jun for a long time, all the way to the train station, on the train, and even after they arrived home in Hohhot.

36

VIOLENCE

The movement had heightened in Hohhot, too. Red Guards were all over the place. Even while walking on the street or going to the department stores, one could run into a group of them chanting their slogans and pushing or dragging a "bad" person with a dunce hat and a banner draped across their chest, both with black inked characters on them. Some banners had a large cross over the person's name. Many of these bad people were older men.

It had been two weeks since Jun took the girls back from Jinzhou. She had gradually established a routine.

On weekdays, a colleague's wife babysat the girls. They called her Aunt Long. On Sundays, Jun kept them home while doing laundry, cleaning, and whatever chores accumulated over the week. Bin-Kai was still at a remote project, and she hardly heard from him. It might be a good thing he was away during this heated moment because who knew what he might have said or done to draw unwanted attention or harsh treatment? A friendly and kind colleague on her team, Wang Hongbao, was suddenly a "bad" person. Two days ago, they dragged him into the canteen. The banner hanging around his neck said, "Knocking down anti-party Wang Hongbao." Rumor said someone reported something he had said earlier in the office.

On this Sunday, Jun put the girls to bed for a nap and laid down next to them and closed her eyes. A loud knock woke up Jun. She got up and walked to the door. From the window, she saw Bin-Nan and Bin-Pei standing outside. Their faces were serious.

This can't be good. She looked back at the soundly sleeping girls, slowly opened the door, stepped out, and closed the door behind her.

Bin-Nan stood there, his hands into fists. He struggled with words and said slowly, "Why did you... How could you take the girls away from our parents?"

"Yeah! When you couldn't take care of them, and didn't even want them!" Bin-Pei followed.

Jun looked at Bin-Pei, "It's not true. I wanted the girls to be together." She turned her face to Bin-Nan and said, "The Red Guards constantly visited your parents. they frightened the girls and may well have traumatized them."

"You've put Ma in bed with a broken heart. She misses the girls. She's been sick ever since." Bin-Nan spilled the words through his teeth.

"You traumatized Ma!" Bin-Pei shouted.

"Shh... The girls are sleeping. Let's move over there." Jun led them away from the door.

"I know it's hard on your family..."

Bin-Nan interrupted her. "Our family? So, you never thought this was your family, too? No wonder you did what you did. A family sticks together no matter what."

"Well, that's your opinion. I still believe the girls are safer here for now. If the situation changes, we can…"

"You can what? Do whatever you want to do? At whatever time you believe is good? Have you ever thought about what others might feel? The way you brought the Red Guards to the house to take the girls away. It was shameful! It was cruel!" Bin-Nan's voice raised.

"What's shameful is your family's class and your mom's attitude toward the Red Guards that only served to antagonize them. It would harm our lives. Not caring about the girls' well-being is cruel," Jun blurted out.

"You consider our family to be shameful? Are you breaking away from our family? Is that what this is about? And not caring about the girls' well-being—what gives you the right to say so? My parents put their hearts into taking care of the girls. You bitch!" Bin-Nan moved one step closer and slapped Jun's face.

Jun covered her face with one hand and looked at Bin-Nan in shock. She couldn't remember ever being beaten by anyone. Before she could say or do anything, Bin-Pei yelled, "You traitor!" and slapped the other side of her face. He kicked her in the legs and punched her in her abdomen.

In the blink of an eye, Jun fell to the ground. She rolled, trying to get up. Bin-Pei kicked her ribs hard and knocked her down again.

Bin-Nan turned her face-up and pinned her to the ground by holding her struggling and fast-moving arms over her head.

Bin-Pei jumped to sit in her middle section, slapping her face and upper body.

Jun cursed as she struggled to free herself. "You bastards! You despicable individuals!"

"YOU are a bastard! A traitor! We'll teach you a lesson," yelled 18-year-old Bin-Pei with each slap. "We'll let you know the consequences of going against our family!"

"Hard! Harder!" hollered Bin-Nan.

"Mama! Mama! Shushu! Stop! Stop!" Lianlian stood by the door, her face covered with tears and her voice trembling as she pleaded repeatedly, "Mama! Mama! Shushu! Stop it! Please stop!"

Bin-Nan turned his face to Lianlian as if to say something. Jun freed up one arm and hit Bin-Nan's face. Blood came out of his nose. He grabbed her arms again and gestured to Bin-Pei to continue.

"Mama! Bad Shushu! Bad Shushu!" Lianlian cried hard. She tried to move forward to help her mom, but she couldn't move her feet. A gush of warm liquid flowed down to her legs and feet.

Shanshan joined Lianlian and screamed hard. "Waaaaa...!"

"Hey! Hey you! Stop! Stop!" Neighbor Lao Kang shouted as soon as he saw them from the top of the stairs. He ran toward them, his face furious. He got hold of Bin-Pei's hand in the air and shouted again, "Stop! Or I'll call the Red Guards! Two men beat a woman in front of babies. How shameful!"

At the top of the stairs, His wife Xiaohe hid her boy in her arms to not let him see the scene. They had just come back from a visit to her parents.

Bin-Pei stopped and stood up. Bin-Nan let go of Jun's arms. They walked to the bottom of the stairway, passed Xiaohe and her boy, and didn't look back.

Jun didn't move. She lay on the ground with her eyes closed. *How long had this beating gone on? Do I still have my arms and legs? Why can't I move them? How strange I don't feel the pain. I don't sense any part of my body. Where are the girls? Are they alright? I don't hear their screaming. Is anyone with them?*

37

WAKING UP

Jun woke up in the hospital. There was excruciating pain in her whole body. She lifted her right hand with effort. It was wrapped with gauze. She touched her face with her left hand and realized her head and arms were in gauze, too. Aunt Long was sitting in a chair next to her bed, knitting. The girls were playing with a piece of yarn on the floor.

"Heeello," Jun made a sound and found her mouth dry.

"You're awake!" Aunt Long rushed to her. "Here, drink some water." She put a spoonful of water in her mouth. Jun pushed the water down through her burning throat.

"Mama! Mama!" The girls jumped up and ran to the bed.

"How long have I been here?"

"Almost 24 hours." Aunt Long continued to feed her water. "Your division head Lao Shao was here during lunchtime. He asked you to see him as soon as you're able. But said don't hurry and take your time to recover."

Jun blinked her eyes.

What would it be about? Oh, that's right. Today is Monday and I'm missing from work.

She moved her legs and arms, and they responded. She lifted her body, sat up, and let out a big yell from the pain. Turning to Aunt Long, she said, "I need to get out of here. Can you get me the doctor?"

Aunt Long ran to get a doctor. Jun used her good hand to touch the cheeks of the babies. They stood by the hospital bed, staring at her intensely. Shanshan stared at her with confusion and alarm, and pointed with a finger, asking, "Your face, Mama?"

Lianlian said nothing. She had a sorrowful look, her mouth set in a frown. Jun could tell Lianlian remembered the beating.

"Hey, my babies. Have you eaten lunch yet?"

"Yeah, a bun bun!" Shanshan waved her hand and tapped her foot.

Lianlian wiped away the tears streaming down her face with her sleeve, her whimpers turning into sobs, despite her best effort to control herself. Shanshan looked at Lianlian and started to cry, too.

"Hush. Shh. Hey, babies, don't cry. Mama will be fine." She used her good hand to wipe the tears from the girls' cheeks and patted their heads.

A doctor came in with a chart and examined Jun.

"How bad is it?" asked Jun.

"You have two broken ribs. They'll take time to heal. You shouldn't lift anything heavy. The cut on your face may leave a scar. You may have a lot of pain in your torn lips. The bruises will take a while to disappear. Wear long sleeves and scarves to cover them. I'm most concerned about any potential damage to your brain because you were out for a long time. We need to observe you for a few more hours. If you remain stable, we can let you go home."

Jun was released from the hospital that evening. Aunt Long kept the girls for the night. Xiaohe brought some food for dinner and a cup of hot water and some pain medicine. Jun slept through the night.

The next morning, Jun wrapped her head with a scarf and knocked on Lao Shao's office door.

Lao Shao helped her sit down and looked carefully at her face. Jun removed the scarf and showed more bruises on her ears, cheeks, and neck. Lao Shao's face changed from shock to concern to anger. "This is a serious matter. You should report it to the police."

Jun sighed, "What will happen to them if I report them?"

"Hard to say these days. In the old days, they would go to jail, and this instance would be in their Dang-Ans."

Authorities would check a person's Dang-An for various reasons, such as job applications, promotion considerations, and other career or daily life matters. Things in the Dang-An stayed there forever unless someone with authority removed them.

Jun thought for a while. She recalled reporting her sister-in-law Meiling to her mom and her classmate Wu Dazhi to her school leader. The consequences of both cases still bothered her. It was hard to know what would happen once the authorities received the report.

I don't want to make things worse. They're young, and their lives could be ruined forever, she reminded herself.

"I don't know. I need to think about it," Jun said slowly.

"You do that. You take a couple of days to decide. But not too long or you lose the window of reporting. Also, take one week off to recover and put your life together. I've requested Bin-Kai to be back as soon as possible."

"Thank you." Jun left the office with a slight relief. She was grateful one of the leaders at the institute was watching over her.

38

CHOICES

Her home looked about the same as two days ago when Jun and the girls were napping, and the girls' uncles had shown up. All the chores from last week were still waiting for Jun. On the counter, a big bowl of dirty clothes was to be washed. The floor needed sweeping. A basket held all the girls' clothes with tears or missing buttons.

Jun's right hand was in gauze. She would have to wait to do the housework. Now, though, she wasn't in the mood—and didn't have the energy—to do anything besides take care of her own basic needs. Everything she needed to do risked others seeing her. The bathroom and cold-water faucets were on the other end of the building. She was hungry and couldn't rely on the crackers meant for the girls. Her neighbor Xiaohe provided some food, but Jun didn't want to bother her too much. People had begun to be cautious when they interacted with each other and Jun vaguely remembered that Xiaohe's parents were in trouble, and that the Red Guards had raided their house, too. But the canteen was quite a walk away and would be full of people at regular mealtimes.

Jun sighed. Her whole body was burning with pain. She needed water to take the pain medicine. But her hot water bottles had been empty for two days. People usually filled their hot water bottles each day by walking across the buildings to the hot water house.

Jun went to the door and listened. People should be at work this time of day. She opened the door and poked her head outside to check, then she hurried to the cold-water faucets and gathered a bucket of water. People believed drinking unboiled water would make them sick. Back at home, she set up the stove and put the water pot on. Minutes later, the pot made a whistling sound. She filled a hot water bottle and a drinking cup.

The medicine worked quickly, and the pain subsided.

Jun sat on the edge of the bed, munching on some crackers. Her mind was buzzing.

How could this have happened? There'd been so much hate and anger in the young men's eyes. Was it true Lao-Si had been sick since I'd taken the girls away?

She hadn't thought about the in-laws up to then—she had been too busy attending to her immediate challenges of working and taking care of the girls. It involved a lot of learning and setting things up. Now, thinking of it, she saw how it must have been an enormous blow to her in-laws. They'd had both girls for a whole year and had raised Shanshan from birth. They'd taken great care of the girls, and their absence must have created an emptiness in their lives.

But what else could I have done? Their home was an ongoing target for the Red Guards, and they didn't consider protecting the girls from those traumatic experiences.

Is it my fault that as a mother I want to keep my babies away from a violent environment? Maybe she'd gone too far by bringing the Red Guards to help her remove the babies. But what else could she have done? The in-laws would never have allowed her to take the girls away. They had protested even with the Red Guards there—though Mr. Zhou had been wise. He seemed to realize the potentially harmful outcome if they went against the Red Guards.

He was indeed a man of vision and strategy. Jun's admiration for Mr. Zhou hiked up a notch.

And what did the two young men come here for? It couldn't be to reason with her. Had they intended to do something else? Had they planned to take the girls away? If so, they might have succeeded if Bin-Nan hadn't lost his temper and hit her. Maybe the beating wasn't part of the plan, and it simply got out of control. If Lao Kang hadn't scared them off, they could have grabbed the girls from the bed while she was lying helplessly on the ground.

Jun had goosebumps all over her body. For the first time in a long while, she felt scared. Who knew what those two young men would do in the future? Would they come back again to take the girls, or to harm her? What would she do if it happened? Should she report them for the beating and put them in jail? But would that happen? Would the beating be enough of a crime to put them away? Lao Shao hadn't seemed sure. So many things were happening at higher levels throughout the country and in the Inner Mongolia region. Personal matters and domestic violence seemed insignificant.

And even if they went to jail, how long would they stay there? What would happen once they got out? They'd have a terrible record that would ruin their chances in life and they'd become her permanent enemies. She'd have to look over her shoulder for the rest of her life.

Did they call me a traitor? Should I become one? Reporting their beating would push her to be a traitor for sure, even if the charge was for the beating, but everyone would know she was cutting her ties with her in-laws. Would this help with her political position and with furthering her career prospects?

The blood beat so hard in Jun's temples she had to press her hands on them, but it didn't help. She took two more pills.

Next to the pill bottle on the table was a photo frame she'd set up a few days ago. On the second day after returning from Jinzhou, Jun had cut the girls' hair short, put on their best clothes—identical overalls Lao-Si had made for them—and took them to a photo shop. *There are no photos of the girls together,* she'd told herself. *Today is a milestone for them. Let this be the evidence of a great start.*

In the photo, Lianlian beamed, and Shanshan had a serious expression. *How different a photo could be from reality.*

Shanshan was the one who was always smiling and laughing, although she sometimes made quiet, sorrowful sounds at night since they left Jinzhou. Maybe she was missing Lao-Si and Mr. Zhou. She could be easily comforted. Give her something and she'd be playing with it for hours without getting bored, only stopping if she was hungry or thirsty. She was a calm baby to care for.

Lianlian was the serious one. Before joining Shanshan in Jinzhou, Lianlian had been content. As long as she could lean on the person she trusted, she was fine and talkative. During visits over the past year, though, Jun had noticed Lianlian becoming quiet, especially in contrast to Shanshan who was front-and-center and everyone's favorite baby. Lianlian said little, didn't make scenes or cause any trouble, and got little attention. She was always excited to see Jun. It surprised Jun when Lianlian mentioned both pleasant and unpleasant things that had happened in the past. Jun had thought babies at two or three years old wouldn't remember anything for very long. But Lianlian remembered. Her tone betrayed which memories made her happy, sad, or envious. Since she'd returned from Jinzhou, Lianlian talked more, even though she was still quite serious most of the time. She trusted Mama and obeyed Mama without question. Lianlian was also a role model for Shanshan, who followed her around and imitated her as much as possible. Lianlian enjoyed taking care of her little sister by dressing and feeding Shanshan, things she'd seen her grandmother do but hadn't gotten to do herself while she'd been in Jinzhou. Jun knew Lianlian had seen terrifying things and that they'd stayed with her—she'd seen the Red Guards attacking her grandparents and her two uncles beating her Mama.

Jun sighed, and wondered how much impact such events would have on Lianlian. In some ways, three-and-a-half-year-old Lianlian was like a young adult.

Jun picked up the picture frame and studied the photo for a long time. She touched the faces of the girls.

What would happen to them if something bad should happen to me?

Jun thought of her upbringing. Things had felt so different after her mom died, even though other family members were still around. Then, after her father died, the sense of family was nonexistent.

Babies need their parents. No one could love or protect them more than their parents, and they won't be the same without their parents. Her mind turned to Bin-Kai.

Where's Bin-Kai? What's happening to him? Does he know what's been going on with his family being targeted by the Red Guards? Does he know I took the girls away? Would he agree with my decision? What would he have done if he'd been there witnessing the Red Guards' raids and how frightened the girls were?

With his frequent and often lengthy absences and Jun's self-reliant nature, she hardly thought of him.

Now she wished he was here. She thought about discovering the torn photo of her and Yanshao—she and Bin-Kai never openly talked about the photo or Jun's relationship with Yanshao. She didn't think it was anything relevant. It was her past, something she tried hard to forget. Now she wished Bin-Kai didn't find the photo.

But it was my past. I have been a faithful wife to him because I love him. I need to see him.

Jun suddenly had a powerful urge to see him and to tell him how she felt about him. She needed him to be here for the girls' sake—they needed their father's presence. She needed him to share the labor of raising the girls, especially right now, when she could hardly take care of herself, let alone the children. If Bin-Kai were there, Jun would feel safe—his brothers wouldn't dare to hurt her.

39

GLUING PIECES

Tump—Tump—Tump—Tump—Tump!

Jun heard the familiar quick steps. She tried to stand up to greet him. But her rib shot through with sharp pain and she let out a loud exhale, bending over and holding her chest. The door rushed open, and she looked up. Bin-Kai towered over the entryway, his hands holding bags. When he saw her, he dropped the bags to the floor and stood there, astonished.

Bin-Kai couldn't believe his eyes. When he was told something bad had happened at home, he'd imagined all kinds of things, but never what he was seeing now before him. Jun looked like a beaten soldier from a war movie, with white gauze wrapped around her. She looked weak, sad, defeated, and in pain.

He went to her, clenching his teeth. "Who did this to you? The Red Guards?" He had received a brief letter from his father about the Red Guards humiliating the family and destroying their belongings. He thought the Red Guards might have found out Jun's relationship to the family and extended their campaign of attacks to include her.

Jun's tears flowed uncontrollably, and Bin-Kai tried to hold her in his arms, but she made a painful sound. Bin-Kai gingerly let go and instead sat down with her. Jun sobbed loudly, finally releasing the physical and emotional pain that had built up inside her over the last few days. Bin-Kai patiently waited.

Jun calmed down. She took a deep breath, then said, "Bin-Nan and Bin-Pei did this to me two days ago."

Bin-Kai's eyes got wide. He stared at Jun wordlessly, unsure if he'd heard her correctly. That wasn't like his brothers at all. They admired him and adored Jun. They'd never dare touch her, let alone attack her this violently.

He swallowed hard and said, "Tell me what happened with as much detail as possible."

"How much do you know about your family's situation?"

"Ba told me the Red Guards visited them and behaved in a very rude manner. That's all. He said I couldn't do much to help and should keep my mind on my work."

Bin-Kai brought her some hot water, and she took a sip. Slowly, she recounted to him what she'd seen during her visits. She explained her reasons for taking the girls away from the chaos, and how she did it, and finally, she described what had happened two days ago.

Bin-Kai didn't interrupt her. He kissed her cheeks softly and wiped her tears from time to time. His tenderness encouraged Jun to continue, to vent out everything inside her.

Bin-Kai said nothing afterward, either. He gently embraced Jun for a long time. There were a lot of things he wanted to say, but he couldn't figure out how. He realized he was in a delicate position, stuck between his family and Jun. But he'd have to ponder that later.

For the moment, he was the primary caregiver for the three ladies in his life. He immediately started doing the chores and brought lunch home from the canteen.

By the end of the day, Aunt Long brought the girls back. It had been a while since the girls had last seen their father. Jun had made more visits than him when the girls were in Jinzhou.

Shanshan exclaimed "Ba Baaa!" and ran toward Bin-Kai as fast as she could. Bin-Kai gathered her up into his arms and kissed her cheeks. He turned to Lianlian, who was standing by the door staring at him. It was hard to tell what was on her mind.

"Come to Baba! Come!" Bin-Kai squatted down, one hand gesturing toward Lianlian and the other holding Shanshan.

Lianlian watched him without moving. It was as if she was gazing at a stranger.

Jun cleared her throat. At the sound, Lianlian turned and rushed to Jun's side, then turned around and watched Bin-Kai again.

Bin-Kai's grin faltered. "I haven't seen the girls for so long that Lianlian has forgotten about me."

Jun put her hand on Lianlian's head. "No, she hasn't. She remembers a lot of things and was traumatized by recent events. She might resent that you weren't here with us when those bad things happened."

Bin-Kai smiled at Lianlian again. "I'll help Mama take care of you two."

Lianlian's face twisted into a frown as tears welled up in her eyes. Before long, her crying became a loud sob. Shanshan cried, too.

Bin-Kai reached for Lianlian's hand and pulled her gently to him. She let him. He picked her up in his other arm and stood up. Holding the two girls, one in each arm, he rocked and danced and sang songs until they both stopped crying.

"Let's go to the canteen to bring food to Mama," Bin-Kai said softly.

Lianlian used the back of her hand to wipe her tears. Her eyes lit up.

"Yeahhh!" Shanshan exclaimed, clapping her hands.

40

ROAD AHEAD

Over the next few days, Jun got steadily better. Her rib pain subsided, although she'd get a sharp reminder from time to time. The gauze bandages were gone. Red bruises over her face, neck, arms, and upper body turned purple, dark yellow, and black. Her lips healed. But the scar on her left cheek became a permanent one. It wasn't outright obvious, but it was noticeable if one looked at her otherwise pretty face for more than a few seconds.

Jun hadn't left the house because she didn't want to let anyone see the way she looked. Fortunately, she didn't have to go out.

Bin-Kai sent the girls to Aunt Long on his way to work, then picked them back up when the workday ended. When he was off work, he was busy taking care of Jun, the girls, the laundry and housekeeping. He was in motion all the time, but he didn't mind.

For Bin-Kai, there was little time to think, and there wasn't much to reason, either. He knew his importance in this young family of four. What had happened had happened. It was too bad he hadn't been there, or things might not have gone this way. But that didn't matter now. He loved his parents and planned to visit as soon as he could. He wanted to have a serious talk with his brothers. They needed to remember that Jun was his wife, no matter what. Plus, they owed Jun a big favor because she cared about them and hadn't pressed charges for the assault.

Whenever he saw the scar on Jun's left cheek, which was daily when they were together, guilt seized him, and his heart sank. He was helpless to reverse what happened in the past. He considered the scar a reminder to treat her nicely to make up for the hurt his brothers had caused her. He never opened up and told Jun these feelings and thoughts, though.

Jun was learning a side of Bin-Kai she'd never known—he was a family man, and a man of few words but plenty of actions. There were times she wished they could discuss what had happened or what the future might hold. But she learned he wasn't that kind of person. He'd rather react and solve problems in the moment than be proactive and plan for the future.

Jun's heart swelled when Bin-Kai was tender toward her and the girls. She was relieved Bin-Kai didn't blame her for anything she'd done. There was no sign Bin-Kai would send the girls back to his parents. Quietly, Bin-Kai agreed with her that the girls should stay here in Hohhot. She knew Bin-Kai would never leave her and the girls and break up their young family. That realization gave Jun the great courage she needed at the moment.

But Bin-Kai didn't openly blame his parents or brothers, either. It was clear to Jun that Bin-Kai wouldn't distance himself from his family. She couldn't guess what his family might do in the future. Jun thought she'd better not count on any help from them.

With Bin-Kai carrying much of the household workload now, Jun had quiet time to think about the girls, her life, and what might lie ahead of her.

Shanshan's face was transparent, revealing whatever she was feeling, and Jun knew how to help cheer her up. It was harder to get a read on Lianlian, who was more of a quiet observer and who had clearly engraved some difficult events onto her memory. Jun's heart broke when she saw clear damage from past events—Lianlian had nightmares frequently ever since they returned from Jinzhou and had wet the bed every night since the beating. Jun had been learning to balance the girls' demands and her workload. Now she realized the girls would need much more of her attention. She had to do her best to take care of them and shield them from further harm of any kind.

Jun thought about the following week when she'd have to return to work. There would have to be some type of explanation in case colleagues asked about her absence or the visible marks on her skin. "Falling down the stairs" would be her answer.

But she worried about work in the weeks, months, or even years ahead. With Bin-Kai absent most of the time, would she have enough strength to take care of the girls and to keep up her star performance and the favorable opinions of her leaders and peers?

Wait a minute. Being a star engineer doesn't mean much if I can't take care of myself and my daughters. Others can cover for me if I'm not at work. But no one can replace me for my girls.

Jun trembled all over with the thought.

With Bin-Kai not always home, my girls have no one to depend on but me. They're my primary responsibility and my top priority. I'm their entire world. And they're mine. I can't bear to see them harmed. I must protect them and provide for them. They're far more important than my career ambitions.

Jun's heart was in turmoil. She knew the road ahead would be bumpy and sensed she was facing another mountain; the highest one she'd faced yet in her life. She recalled what her father said to her: "Junjun always wants to climb to the top of any mountain in front of her."

Ba, you knew me well. Watch over me, help me overcome this mountain.

Jun closed her eyes and sent a prayer to her beloved father in heaven.

<div align="center">~~~ To be continued ~~~</div>

Dear Reader: The stories of the main characters continue in another book, and mainly from Lianlian's perspective: ***Daughter of Blue City: A Novel of Coming-of-Age Through Revolutionary China***. Its prologue is at the end of this book.

Reading Group Discussion Questions

(More can be found at AppleAnBooks.com)

General Questions

1. What did you like best about ***Mother of Red Mountains***, and what did you like least? Why?

2. Which aspects of the book do you feel like you can personally relate to?

3. Do you feel a connection with a particular character? If so, who, and why?

Questions on Content

1. What have you learned from the book about China's history and politics? How is what you've learned consistent with, or different from, what you understood about China before you read the book?

2. The book covers many events that took place between the 1930s and 1966 that were important in shaping Jun's life. Some of these occurred at national and regional levels, and some took place locally or within the family. Which

moments do you think most influenced the development of Jun's character and temperament? Which moment or event do you think was the most important turning point in Jun's life? Why?

3. Which characters played an important role in Jun's life at different stages?

4. How do you feel about Jun and Yanshao's relationship? If you were in Jun's situation, would you make similar decisions? Why or why not?

5. Compare the various women in the book such as Mrs. Liu, Lao-Si, Sanyi, Jun, Xia, Peifang, and Jun's friends. What do these women have in common?

6. The Zhou family were deemed "capitalists." Do you think they were good, evil, or normal people? What are your thoughts about the demonization of capitalism at this time and place?

7. How do you feel about the relationship between Jun and Bin-Kai? Was Bin-Kai an ideal husband? What do you think their future holds? Will their relationship stay strong?

8. At what moment did Jun's motherly instincts wake up and make her act differently?

9. What do you think the two baby girls' future lives will be

like?

10. Do the stories in the book remind you of your childhood, or the childhoods of people you know? Do these stories have universal meanings?

11. The story explores several overarching themes, and Jun and the other main characters learn some important lessons. How did the author bring these themes and lessons to life?

12. The book's title has mountains in it. Do you think the mountains are effective metaphors for the different eras and challenges which Jun and many other Chinese were facing at the time? Would you have given the book a different title?

Questions on Writing

1. What makes this book engaging? Are there places you felt lost or needed more information? Was this because of the writing, or because of your unfamiliarity with what was happening in China during that period?

2. The structure of this historical novel is largely chronological. Is this effective at showing the ever-changing environments, Jun's observations and reflections, and the overall story of what happened during the time?

3. This historical novel is based on actual events. The main characters are fictionalized but they, too, are based on real people. Do you think the stories and characters, as well as their thoughts, actions, and emotions, are realistic? If so,

what has the author done to achieve that realism? If not, how could the author have helped bring them more to life?

4. Are the socio-political events effectively blended into the narration to provide contexts and settings? How well does the author portray the impacts of these events?

5. What do you think were the author's goals when they wrote this book?

6. If you could chat with the author, what would you ask?

Dear Reader

If you enjoyed this book, please leave a review to help other readers decide if this is a book they will enjoy.

If you would like to read more of Apple's literary journey, including news, updates, freebies, media coverages, etc., please sign up for her free newsletters at https://appleanbooks.substack.com/ or with the following QR code.

Apple An's Book Bytes
(AABB) Newsletters

Thank you!

Daughter of Blue City

Prologue

I t was 1977 in Hohhot, the capital of China's Inner Mongolia Autonomous Region. Early fall was a favorite season for the locals—neither hot nor humid, with sunshine filling the long days.

Joyful anticipation filled the air as people looked forward to the positive changes following the end of China's Cultural Revolution a year earlier.

A railroad worker had noticed a particular teenage girl twice now in the late afternoons. She was skinny, dressed in oversized clothes handed down by grown-ups. A schoolbag slung across her body showed she was coming from school. Her two braided pigtails were a typical hairstyle for young girls.

The girl walked along the tracks. He had seen her yesterday and wanted to warn her to stay away, but a co-worker called him away. Before he could get back to her, she had vanished.

Today, he wanted to make sure he reached out and talked to her.

"Hey, young lady, stay right where you are!" The worker hurried toward her, one hand holding the wrench he used to inspect the tracks, the other holding his protective helmet.

The girl paused and turned. Her gaze was vague, fixed on a distant point.

The worker took a deep breath—her face showed no fear, only deep sadness. Something heavy weighed on her mind.

"What are you doing here?" he asked.

The girl snapped back to the here and now; her expression shifted from sad and desperate to alert. She replied, "Just walking."

"How did you get in here? This area is dangerous; it's for workers only."

She pointed at the large metal gate for moving luggage carts.

"Through there," she blushed.

"Little girl, what's your name?" the worker asked, his tone free of blame and full of concern.

The girl looked at him, hesitating, then replied softly, "Zhou Lianlian. My name is Zhou Lianlian."

"Zhou Lianlian, which school do you attend? Which grade?"

The girl still showed no fear. His kind expression and gentle tone must have assured her he was trustworthy.

"Hohhot 2nd Middle School. I've just started the third year."

The worker thought she was small for that grade. "That is 25 minutes from here. Where do you live?"

The girl took a slow, steady breath before responding. "About five minutes from here," she said, adjusting her schoolbag to give her right shoulder a moment's relief.

"I... I used to come here to watch the trains with my sister."

The worker nodded and looked her over carefully. He believed she was telling the truth, and his voice became even gentler.

"You should go home now. This is not a place for members of the public. Last week's accident caused us a lot of grief. Poor boy. He would still be alive if he hadn't come here to play with his buddy. You must have heard about the accident?"

The girl nodded, glancing down at her feet for a moment before lifting her head. "Sorry to cause you concern. I was just walking and thinking. I'll go home now," she said.

"Good. Don't come back again. Let me lead you to the gate."

From the multi-award-winning author

Apple An

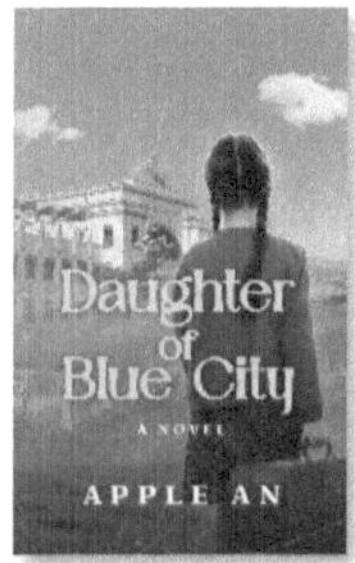

Visit AppleAnBooks.com

Voices Heard Publishing, LLC

Daughter of Blue City

A Novel of Coming-of-Age Through Revolutionary China
© 2025

In the turmoil of China's Cultural Revolution, young Lianlian's life shattered by family violence, public shame, and crushing poverty. Raise by a resilient but scarred mother, shadowed by an abusive father, an anchored by a little sister, Lianlian learns to survive a life with a impossible future. When the political climate shifts, she discovers th her mind is her only weapon and education is her only hope. Fueled b fierce determination and the quiet support of her mother, Lianlian battle for a spot at a top university, seeing it as her one true path to a life sh can call her own.

If you like books about Chinese culture by **Amy Tan, Lisa See**, an **Pearl S. Buck**, and books about coming-of-age such as ***A Tree Grows i Brooklyn*** by **Betty Smith**, you will like this book!

*"A deeply moving coming-of-age novel." – **Derrick Mead***

*"Impossible to put down." – **TQ Pu***

*"What touched me most was how her mother and sister gave her qui strength." – **Sammy Moo***

Las Crosses

An Unwavering Journey to a New Life in America © 2023

eing the aftermath of the Tiananmen Square crackdown in 1989 and
led by a burning desire for a better life, Apple embarks on a daring
rney to pursue her doctoral education in America. With no backup
n, Apple must make this journey work. But she has no idea that her
rting place, Las Cruces, NM, is a quiet desert town - a far cry from the
tling metropolis she envisioned. Anxious, ignorant, and homesick,
ple faces challenges she never had before. But she is determined to be
n-minded. Excited and curious, will she simply survive the fish-out-
the-water situation many immigrants experience, or will she thrive in
unexpected American adventure?

*story of opportunity, bravery and self-invention that's as suspenseful
and inspiring as it is quintessentially American."* - **Jonathan Dee**

*"Powerfully depicts scenes, characters, and emotions with bits of
comedy." -* **Cate McGowen**

*n enjoyable and essential read on cultural contrast from a historical
era." -* **Ginnah Howard**

*An inspiring story of resilience, hope and joyful curiosity, even in the
face of uncertainty and difficulty. Uplifting!" –* **Diane Pienta**

37 More Voices

Voices Heard Anthology Series, Vol. 2 © 2025

Beyond the everyday, what hidden wisdom awaits in the tapestry of
lives? Picking up where Volume 1, **28 Voices**, left off, this captivati
second collection of essays invites you on a profound exploration
discovery and reflection.

Through a diverse array of personal narratives, these pages delve into
myriad ways we learn and grow. From the quiet revelations of se
awareness to the complex dynamics of family and friendship, disco
the profound impact of connection. Uncover unexpected insights fro
the loyalty of pets, the discipline of hobbies, and the expans
perspectives gained from travel and exploration. Ultimately, these essa
illuminate how every experience—large or small—contributes to
ever-evolving landscape of our personal philosophies and worldview

Join us on a journey of introspection that celebrates the richness of lif
lessons, beautifully told.

28 Voices

Voices Heard Anthology Series, Vol. 1 © 2024

very life is a story, and every story holds a lesson. Within these 28 timate essays, a diverse group of authors invites you to witness their ost defining moments. They recount the laughter and pain of childhood emories, the forks in the road that marked life-changing events, and the art's journey through love and relationships. Feel the awe of childbirth d parenthood, the struggle of balancing family and professional nbition, and the courage it takes to adapt to a new culture. With raw nesty, they explore the quiet resilience found in coping with losses and e personal paths to spirituality. These 28 honest reflections on the urney of life is a testament to what we can all learn, and what we have give.

*"Not gonna lie, some of these short stories really got to me. They're worth checking, just prepare yourself." - **Paul Hoon***

*"Some of these stories are difficult to get through due to the nature of the stories, but overall the anthology was a good read." - **Jake Jacob***

*Written by ordinary people leading ordinary lives. How very relatable it is. I was enthralled by the talent that was gathered together to contribute to this book. I enjoyed it completely and I strongly recommend it." - **Shannon Brennan***

All-in-One Dotted Journal Notebook

For a Busy, Productive & Mindful Life © 2023

Planners + Organizers + To-dos + Reminders + Trackers + Journals + Random Notes + Doodles + Nuggets of Goodness.

Do you have a busy life? Do you want to be productive? Do you want to have an efficient assistant to provide notes when you need it? Do you want to eliminate loose papers and memos? Do you want to have fewer notebooks or journals to deal with daily? Do you want to spend minimum time preparing your templates and more time to be productive and enjoy life? This All-in-One Dotted Journal Notebook might be just what you need.

Give this a try for one month. There is no need to waste money if it does not work for you. You can find examples to guide you to developing your own habits and uses.

"Takes getting organized to a new level!" - **Joseph Brennan**

"I absolutely love this planner! If you're looking for an efficient planner, this is worth considering." - **Angela Dorr**

"I appreciate most about this notebook is the upfront guidance and examples. It inspired me to use the notebook in ways I never would have thought of." - **Leon Edwards**

"I am pleased with the large number of flexible templates for my various needs." - **Kateryna Hlushchenko**

About the Author

Apple An is an award-winning author and professor whose stories explore migration, cultural memory, and the quiet strength of women through times of upheaval. She writes under her pen name to celebrate her Chinese heritage and share universal truths. Apple lives in New York State, where she balances storytelling, scholarship, and a lifelong love of movement and learning. Learn more about Apple An and her creative work at AppleAnBooks.com.

www.ingramcontent.com/pod-product-compliance
Lightning Source LLC
Chambersburg PA
CBHW061343310726
48974CB00001B/181